T0113602

MOSTLY TRUE

Stories of Growing, Life, Side Trips, Travel, Volcanoes and Redheads

(Originally published in Island Park News)

DICK MARLER

authorHOUSE®

AuthorHouse™
1663 Liberty Drive
Bloomington, IN 47403
www.authorhouse.com
Phone: 1 (800) 839-8640

Published by AuthorHouse 11/15/2016

ISBN: 978-1-5246-5022-3 (sc)
ISBN: 978-1-5246-5021-6 (e)

Library of Congress Control Number: 2016919191

Print information available on the last page.

This book is printed on acid-free paper.

Introduction

Ann Marie Anthony
Owner/Editor
Island Park News

What can I say about someone who has lived his
whole life and put most everyday happenings
into words. He is one of those souls who
you feel like you have known forever.

Dick's ability to see the humor in everyday occurrences
makes it a joy to know him and love him. I love all
of his stories and I know you will too. So join me in
reading, enjoying and laughing at the everyday life
details of Dick and Sharon, his redhead bride.

Prepare to be entertained.

Author's Note

Many years ago I was reading an article in the Island Park News. I can't remember what it was about, or why it caught my attention. I do know that I was driven to write a letter to the editor. A week later I wrote another one, then another one, and after a while I was afraid I was writing too many and called; I talked to a nice lady who asked if I could do it every week, and that's how it started.

Almost 20 years later, the Redhead said she was going to put my stories in a book, and here it is. You may find typos and maybe even some creative spelling, That happens. But these are the ghost stories that have shaped my life. I hope you enjoy reading them. They are who I am.

Without the support of my wife Sharon, and the former editor of the Island Park News, Elizabeth Laden, this would have never have come to be. I would also to thank the current editor of the paper, Ann Marie Anthony for her support, and the decision to keep me.

Preface

My wife and daughters asked me to write my story so my grandchildren and great-grandchildren would know me, who I was, and what I believed to be true.

This request led me back to my childhood where I was told stories by my father and have included Pa's wisdom in many of my own stories.

These stories stay close to me like a ghost from my past. They have helped me in daily life, in my thoughts and actions.

I hope you will find your own ghost stories and record them to pass on within your family. They are important.

A little note from the author...

I hope you enjoy my stories. Yes, may find a typo now and then, and maybe some creative spelling, but these are the ghost stories that have shaped my life. They are who I am.

Table of Contents

Let the stories begin...

Remember Stories

It is starting to look a little bit like spring. At least it is down here in the lowlands. Looking north towards the mountains it still looks like the dead of winter.

Spring is a good time of year. Everything is new, the grass doesn't need to be mowed yet, there is nothing in the garden to water, and the dogs can let themselves outside to do what ever it is they do when they go outside.

Early spring, like today, is a good time to start planning trips to Yellowstone so I can be in one of the first automobiles to make the drive along the Madison River and hopefully watch an elk of two scratch away the last remnants of snow looking for a taste of fresh grass. Who knows, I might even get to see a real wild bison before they all disappear into a zoo or commercial ranch where they will join cows in their life long quest to become hamburger or jerky.

Don't worry, I'm not going to get all maudlin and politically rabid about bison control. We

all know where it's heading and there is nothing we can do to stop it. Unless, of course, we can teach bison not to eat grass so the cows can have it all. I mean, think about it. What is more important than a thick beefsteak covered with mushrooms and onions? Certainly not a bison that may or may not have some kind of disease or something!

Well, there is one thing I can do. I can collect memories, and no one can stop that. When the time comes, I will be able to share my memories about a time when it was possible to watch wild bison swim across the Madison River while teaching their young to face their fears and trust their instinct. I don't know if they know it or not but I know that they have been swimming across this same river for thousands of years. That's something to think about, isn't it?

I like to think about Yellowstone as being more than just a park or wildlife refuge. I like to think of Yellowstone as being the memory of the earth. It remembers the time when a great explosion occurred that sent ash around the world. It remembers when great glaciers came out of the mountains covering the park with ice thousands of feet deep. Yellowstone remembers when the ground slowly rose up and rivers cut down through it creating a huge canyon and thundering waterfalls.

Yellowstone not only remembers, she tells us stories. If you sit quietly in the trees you can hear stories about great herds of bison grazing along the Lamar River and grizzly bears so huge they could block out the sun. One of my favorites is her story about the trees that got so old they turned to stone. Another is all about the millions of visitors who come to visit every year.

Things are changing in Yellowstone. A new kind of visitor and new kinds of campers are Coming to the Park. Hot pools are drying up and new ones are being born.

There are so many changes I can't keep up. But that's okay. I will be there when the summer season begins, listening for new stories of what took place during the winter.

Change is part of the natural order. I intend to witness as much of it as I can, then tell the stories to whoever will listen.

A Boy and His Dog

There is an acknowledged law of nature that establishes an invisible bond between objects that otherwise would fly around aimlessly, creating chaos in the universe. Planets are connected to their stars, moons to their planets, and boys to their dogs. That's just the way it is, and there is nothing we can do about it.

Think of the bedlam at the coffee shop if all the dogs in the back of the pickups decided to change places with each other. Most of the guys at the counter have a difficult enough time in maintaining their spatial relationship with the cosmos when they find someone else sitting on their stool.

Can you just imagine the confusion when they can't find their pickup in the parking lot because there is a poodle in the back instead of a pit bull?

The thing is, boys are very attached to their dogs and consider them an extension of the self. This bond is so profound that in most cases it is hard to distinguish one from the other. A friendly guy will own a friendly dog; a less then friendly guy will attach himself to a dog that is a bit of a grouch himself. Hunters will own labs and farmers will hang out with Australian shepherds. I'm not sure what kind of a dog it is that hooks up with cowboys, but then, maybe cowboys aren't sure what they are either.

As for myself, I don't own a dog. We do have a dog that lives with us; however, she belongs to the Redhead. Sure, I'm the one who makes sure her food bowl is full and that she has water to drink when she needs it. And if she doesn't make it outside in time, I'm the one who takes care of her little accidents. But she is not mine!

Just because she thinks my lap is a magical futon that appears every time I sit down to watch television and I'm the person who replaces the little pink bows in her hair when they fall out, doesn't mean that there is any kind of bonding going on between us. Trust me, if I owned a dog it would be an Irish setter, not a ShihTzu.

Of course there are a couple advantages to having a dog that doesn't quite weigh ten pounds. She takes up very little space on the bed and I'm certainly thankful she's not a St. Bernard when she wakes me up in the middle of the night to go out by sitting on my head. And, when I take her for walks, I have an opportunity to meet a lot of people who otherwise wouldn't take the time to say "Hi."

5

If you spot me around the neighborhood, walking with a little ball of fluff that has pink ribbons in her hair, please don't assume that she is an extension of my self. She belongs to the Redhead, even if nobody remembered to tell her that.

She is cute though! But then, so is the Redhead.

My Victory Garden

I was crawling around the floor during WW2, and coming of age during the Korean mess, I got used to there being a garden in the back yard. Pa called it his Victory Garden and I always assumed that the victory was making anything grow in the hardpan soil that passed for dirt out by the alley that ran behind the house.

By the time I was big enough to stand on my own, Pa let me ride on the push plow while he turned every thing over getting ready for spring planting. It wasn't until much later in life that I found out he was looking for a little bit of weight to help the plow dig deep into the earth. After the rows were neatly prepared, he would let me follow behind him while he planted corn, beets, carrots, squash and spuds. My job was to gently cover each seed with a little bit of dirt and pat it down just a bit. I got it right some of the time, but Pa usually had to go back and reshape the rows into straight lines and fix the flat spots left by knees so the water would be able to flow in the right direction.

When the time was right, we would go to the garden and pick all the ripe corn, beets, carrots and squash, and Mom would put it all in quart jars to be stored in the basement until they were needed.

The spuds were left in the ground until after the first frost came; then we would dig them up, put them in sacks and carry them to the basement where they would spend the winter on the floor next to the quart jars.

It wasn't until I was grown that I learned Victory Gardens were planted to help with the war effort because most of the fresh vegetables were being sent to the front lines to feed the solders that were fighting to keep us free. Of course, what was available in the stores was rationed and required food stamps to make a purchase.

Even with this kind of bringing up, I am not a gardener. I have tried several times over the years but haven't ever been able to grow enough of anything for a light snack, let alone enough to fill a quart jar. But now that I'm retired and have a lot of time on my hands, I decided to give it another try.

I measured the area I have available for planting, drew a map of what I wanted to plant where, and even went out back and made a list of things I needed to do to get ready for spring planting. The list included such things as clear the brush, plow up the ground, lay out the rows, and figure out how to get water out of the ditch on the other side of the fence. That's a lot to do!

When the time came, I gave careful consideration to all my options and decided the best thing for me to do would be to plant everything in boxes so I wouldn't have to dig up much brush, make it easer to pull the weeds, and forget about planting corn all together. I also forgot to build the boxes, buy the seeds, and actually plant the garden.

I found a couple garden boxes at a yard sale last week, and have some big bags of peat moss and vermiculite left over from last year when I was getting ready to plant.

All I need now is enough dirt to fill the boxes and I'm ready to go. Of course, I'm going to have to wait until next spring after the last frost to start planting seeds. Pa's Victory Garden may have helped bring the end to a war, but my garden will bring an end to the Redhead's constant reminders that she wants a fresh salad for supper.

Memorial Day

Decoration Day has been observed since the end of the Civil War to honor the Union Soldiers who gave their lives to preserve United States of America. Over time the date has changed, as has the name. Towards the end of the 19th century many people started using the name Memorial Day but it wasn't until 1967 that congress made Memorial Day official. In 1971 the last Monday in May was designated as a federal holiday.

Bringing up this short piece of history is my feeble attempt to help those who celebrate Memorial Day as nothing more than the first day of the vacation season, and forgotten about the hundreds of thousands men and women who gave their lives to preserve the Union, and have made it possible for us to live in the proudest, and free nation on earth.

Like most families, we, as Americans, may fight amongst each other over trivial and important issues, but we come together as one whenever the nation is attacked or threatened. I remember the outburst of patriotism that occurred after the attacks on September 9th. 2001. It didn't matter what slogan was displayed on the bumper of our trucks, flags flew proudly from our radio antennas.

Differences in religious beliefs were replaced with a common prayer for help and guidance to cope with the loss of the 2000 plus who died in the attack. Opposing Political ideologies were temporarily put on hold as our leaders struggled with the challenges of preparing and taking action necessary to keep us safe and free.

Throughout our nations history we have been faced with the similar challenges, and have responded with the same vigor that we did then. Not long after our nation was established we were faced with another war against the British. We came together to protect our new nation. When American interests in Cuba and the Philippines were threatened by Spain, we fought our first two-ocean war. In the early 1900s we left our shores to offer aid to our friends, and former enemies, to free them from the iron hand of German Oppression, and a little over thirty years later we did it again. We can all stand proud in the shadow of the men and women of our military forces who served, and gave their lives for out freedoms.

Today, at this very minute we have again called on our military personnel to leave their homes and families, with no assurance that they will return, and offer them our thank you when they do.

Please, let's all take at least a minute or so out of our busy lives and remember all those who made the sacrifice to keep us free. If you can, count the flags on the graves of our fallen veterans, and remember that with out them, we would not be here.

First Day

Winters may be long and they may be cold, and some years they seem to last forever.

Actually, all winters seem to last forever no matter how harsh or mild they are and from a useful sense, it makes no difference to me if the temperature outside is ten degrees or minus ten degrees, it's still cold.

It doesn't matter if there is a couple inches of snow in the driveway or a couple of feet, it still has to be cleared away before the Redhead can get her car out of the garage. Of course, the very best thing about winter is that no matter how bad it gets, you know it's going to end eventually.

For the Redhead and myself, winter officially ended this weekend with the official opening of the roads in Yellowstone National Park.

For reasons I don't care to get into right now, our trips to Yellowstone are going to be greatly curtailed this year so we decided to make the best of it and leave early Friday morning and not come home until late Monday night. We would have stayed longer but her dog has an appointment with the groomer on Tuesday and there are priorities.

Before leaving home I checked the weather online and was a bit disappointed to see the four-day forecast was calling for thunderstorms and heavy rain. Of course, I have been on the planet long enough not to believe everything I hear about the weather and was not at all surprised that we had three great days of sunshine and warm temperatures.

We got to see how well the elk around Mammoth Hot Springs had survived the winter, and we saw more bison munching the grass in Lamar Valley than we have seen in quite a while. They haven't started calving yet, so I guess we will have to wait until next year to watch the little redheads test each other out to see who can run the fastest.

No bears, no wolves, only a couple really fat coyotes hunting along the banks of the Madison River munching on mice, ground squirrels, and any other small furry critters they could find.

We did get to watch a river otter catching fish in the Lamar River. That was something I haven't seen in a very long time, and it got real exciting when he stuck his head out of the water, looked me straight in the eye and said hello.

Maybe that was his way of letting me know that even if it's going to be a while before we get back, he and everyone else will be here waiting. That is nice to know.

So long for now...we will be back.

The Sandhillsare Back

Last fall, the Sandhill Cranes that had been living in the fields west of my house, packed their bags and headed south for the winter.

This annual migration pretty much follows the same path as many of the human residents of Yellowstone country. When the temperatures start to drop and the smell of early snow begins to fill the air, they load up their Winnebago's, board up their cabins, and set out for warmer places in Arizona and New Mexico. Some may stop in southern Utah, while others keep going further south to Mexico. In any case, none of them will spend much time shoveling snow off the sidewalks, or chipping ice off of windshields.

While they are enjoying their winter retreats under the desert sun sipping fruit flavored Daiquiris and Mimosas, the rest of us were gassing up our snow machines, waxing our skies, and pretending that we love the cold and we love the snow.

The truth be told, when the temperature drops below the O mark on the thermometer hanging on the tree in back of the house, most of us who stay here waste a lot of time day dreaming about palm trees and blue skies while waiting for the water to heat up so we can make one more cup of hot chocolate. Sweetened with a splash of brandy and decorated with marshmallows of course.

Studies have shown that the human body can only tolerate so much hot chocolate, coupled with not hearing the distinctive bark of the cranes. An overdose of either, or both, is sure to bring on the dreaded malady of SAD. SAD is a nationally recognized acronym for Sandhills Arrival Delays.

SAD symptoms can manifest themselves by a person staring blankly at the early morning horizon as if looking for something to appear, and cupping of the ears in a vain attempt to magnify sound.

This is generally followed by a frantic search on the computer for Yellowstone web cams, followed by watching a live feed of the steam rising from Old Faithful geyser on the monitor, and hoping to see a bear or bison stroll past the empty benches on the walk way.

Early this morning I was in the back yard waiting for the redhead's dog to find the right spot to take care of her business when I heard the distinctive sound of newly arrived cranes announcing their return coming from the fields next door.

There they were, two of them. They were bobbing their heads and jumping high in the air in an apparent dance of joy for being home. Of course, what they were really doing was displaying doctor, do you come here often?"

What ever it was they were doing, they are back. Spring is in the air, and the park opens in just a few weeks.

I guess winter wasn't all that bad after all.

Abandoned

I have a daughter who chooses to live in California on purpose who volunteers for an animal rescue organization that advocates the adoption of lost and neglected pets. In her zeal to educate the world about the plight of four legged homeless critters, I have been bombarded with more information about the cruelty of humans towards animals than need to know.

I'm not complaining, mind you; I am very proud of what she is doing. I think that all of us have an obligation to do what we can to help ease the suffering and loneliness of these unfortunate creatures.

However, there is another class of neglected and abandoned pets that no one seems to care about or even notice. You won't see any television specials delving deep into their most inner secrets in an attempt to foster understanding. You won't hear of any outreach organizations asking for a monetary contribution to help them deal with the demons that plague their souls.

What you will find is groups of one of more of these solitary creatures perched on a stool at the local coffee shop staring blankly into an empty cup wishing it were full.

When approached, they will put on a brave face and make jokes about "being without adult supervision," or tell wild stories about being able to stay up late watching the History Channel special on the Crimean war.

Oh yeah, let's not forget that without supervision, they get to sleep in as late as they want, and wander around the house in their underwear if they choose and if the blinds are pulled.

The reality is, none of them are that interested in obscure events in European history nor would they dare not to put on a pair of trousers when getting out of bed. Sleeping late is defined as "getting up early" to get the dishes done, and picking up dirty socks and retrieving carelessly tossed towels from behind the couch, just in case she comes home early.

If you're interested in how I seem to know so much about neglected and abandoned husbands, it is because I am one. Don't feel sorry for me, I had it coming. After years of leaving the Redhead behind for days, weeks, or even months at a time, it's only natural that she should take off for a few days with friends and travel to Montana to attend some who left their husbands behind to fend for themselves. At least all I had to take care of in her absence was the dog, the laundry, the dishes, the vacuuming, bed making, and toilet scrubbing.

She is back now, and I will have to admit that it's kind of nice to be reminded that I have no real interest in the Crimean war, and that if I go to bed early I will wake up sooner and can go over to the coffee shop, sit on a stool staring blankly into a half-full cup and brag to no one special about how great it was to be without adult supervision.

Gardening

I am not a gardener and never have been. When the Redhead and I were living in Tennessee, I tried to grow tomatoes. After preparing the ground with the right amount of dirt, peat moss, and other expensive stuff the guy at the seed store told me I needed to grow a good garden, I planted a tomato bush. All summer long I insured that it was fertilized, de-bugged, and well watered. After following all the tips and suggestions that kept coming from my neighbors and friends, a tomato began to bud, then grow.

When I was a kid, everyone I knew had a "Victory" garden in his backyard. Because of the war, everything was rationed and fresh vegetables just couldn't be found in the local grocery store. During the summer months all our veggies came direct from the garden to the table; in the fall they went directly into quart jars that were stacked neatly on shelves in the basement so we could eat them during the winter. It was a great way to get cheap food, eat healthy, and help with the economic recovery after the war ended.

After leaving home and going out into the world on my own, I discovered that I could walk into almost any store, and find shelves of canned veggies of just about every sort. Corn, beans, peas, beets, and even squash were available all year if you had access to a can opener. Even things I had never heard of, let alone had for supper. Things like okra, chili peppers, artichokes and capers. I still don't know what a caper is, but it goes well with garlic butter on spaghetti. Of course, you must add fresh tomatoes, right off the vine.

I'm not sure why I decided to try my hand at gardening when we were in Memphis. Maybe I wanted to set an example of self-sufficiency for the girls. I don't know! I knew that an example only works when it works, so I started out small. One plant couldn't be that hard to deal with, and success was all but assured.

What wasn't assured was how many tomatoes one plant was going to produce. In my case, one plant equaled one tomato. One BIG tomato! But still, just o

After factoring in the cost of the dirt, fertilizer, bug spray and the little basket thingy I bought to hang my tomato on the fence with, that lonely little tomato cost me somewhere

in the neighborhood of 75 dollars. And, it didn't taste all that good either.

That is why I was surprised when last week the Redhead suggested that I plant a garden. This time she wants tomatoes, beans, peas, carrots, cabbage, and a bunch of other stuff I can get from the store, and keep my hands clean in the process.

But, being a good little soldier, I agreed and started getting together the stuff I was going to need to do a "Four Foot Garden. To make it short, a four-foot garden is fool proof and has guaranteed results.

I certainly hope so! So far I have invested $40 for the boxes the garden will grow in, $160 for the special dirt and stuff the veggies will need to flourish, and another $10 dollars for incidentals. I haven't bought any seeds or plants yet, but I sure do hope what ever happens I will get at least two tomatoes out of my investment.

My Addiction

Unlike my friends who live up the mountain, I have more grass in my yard than I do snow. The truth be known, the only snow I have left is part of the piles that built up when I had my roof shoveled a couple months ago, and that should be gone by the end of the week. It's probably best if I don't tell a lot of people about spring finally coming into my life; I wouldn't want anyone to think I'm gloating, even if I am.

There is only one serious issue I have with the onset of nicer weather; it seems to show up well before Yellowstone National Park opens gates for over the road travel. That means that I have to sit at home doing nothing except fantasize about the clear roads with no cars full of tourists, bears feeding on winter kill ten yards away from the asphalt, and giant bull elk that haven't dropped their antlers yet, grazing next to the river.

Sure, there's probably still a bit of snow blocking access to most of the picnic areas, and travel may be a bit difficult on the mountain passes. It wouldn't surprise me any to find out that getting from Old Faithful to Lakeside is next to impossible. I have a friend who works for the park service that has been assuring me that they are working real hard to get everything ready for me. But he always adds some sort of discouraging comment about not being able promise anything due to not being able to control the weather.

If the weather is good here, I see no reason why it should be any different inside the boundaries of the park. After all, isn't Yellowstone federal land controlled by a federal agency? The feds control almost everything else in my life, why shouldn't they be willing to insure that nothing will interfere with my upcoming trip to celebrate opening day.

In fact, why can't Congress just pass a law prohibiting any snow on the ground after the first day of March, and that Yellowstone be open to over the road travel for me, and anyone who might be riding in my car.

Believe me, I'm not trying to be greedy or anything, I'm perfectly able to share the park with almost anyone. I'm just not willing to share it until after I have had my first spring fix. It has been a long time since I have experienced the surge of adrenalin that comes with looking across Lamar Valley and believing that you are seeing into a world that existed tens of thousands of years ago.

It's hard to explain to a non-addict why the need to experience one more trip can be more important than deciding what to fix for supper.

But like all addicts, I know that all will be well just as soon as I can see the gate at West Yellowstone disappear into my rear view mirror. The Redhead and I will be heading for our first stop somewhere along the Madison River where we plan to do nothing except sit quietly, breathe the air, and watch the water flow by.

We're not going to spend all our time doing nothing. After the initial rush of our first look at Madison Junction, where the park was born, we will be taking a leisurely drive to Mammoth Hot Springs, then into the city of Gardiner Montana. We have been told that there is going to be a YAA, (Yellowstone Addicts Anonymous) meeting, at a local eatery where we can all share our first day in the park, and congratulate each other for surviving the winter.

"Hello, my name is Dick, and I love Yellowstone."

April Fools

There is an old story that comes around every year about this time. I don't know why but every time I hear it, I'm surprised that I hadn't heard it before. I am even more surprised when I remember that I have heard it dozens of times. It's probably a good thing I can't remember it for more than a few days at a time because that way I get to laugh at it all over again.

It seems that when God created the world He promised women that they would be able to find a good man by searching the four corners of the earth. Then, he made it round! Even God can appreciate a good April Fools joke.

Growing up in a house full of boys, I always believed that the second prank had something to do with pulling Pa's finger. With my first experience in finger pulling behind me, I began to understand that the aftermath wasn't all that funny. And besides, my much older brothers liked to play the same game over and over again, no matter what day it was. Of course, the outcome of the game would invariably get Ma a little testy, and that was never a good thing.

One of the best April Fools' pranks that my friend Jim and I ever pulled had something to do with a ground up Alka-Seltzer, a bowl of sugar, and his dad's morning coffee. I thought it was funny, Jim thought it was funny. Even his snooty sister thought it was funny. Mama C, that's what we called Jim's mother, didn't think it was funny at all. I think we all learned that watching someone's morning beverage foam and bubble all over the kitchen table was not a good thing.

A good thing was when my girls were little and we were living in the deserts of Nevada. The Redhead and I would get up early and start giggling and yelling about all the snow that fell the night before. At the time, the girls had never seen snow and got real excited about going out side and playing in it. I thought it was funny, the Redhead thought it was funny, but even three and four year olds are capable of hate stares when they find out that the ground was white from alkali that had leached up from the sand and not snow: Oh Well!

I can appreciate a good prank now and then. I like to pull them, and I like to have them pulled on me. I still don't like pulling fingers.

I even refused to pull the Redhead's toe once when she was having a cramp.

I can appreciate the fact that April Fools' Day is celebrated during the first part of spring. Maybe after a long winter with all the snow, cold weather, and gray skies that have lasted a gazillion months, we need to laugh at something, even if it is at each other.

What we don't need is to get all excited when grass begins to show up around the edges of the yard only to have it snow again while we were sleeping. The weather, evidently, is another prank.

That's an April Fools joke I really didn't need.

Happy New Year

It's hard to believe that December is almost over and we are still waiting around for the snow to come. There is a little bit here, and a little bit there, but not a whole lot anywhere. At least not as much snow as we should have this time of year. I know it's a bit tacky to rhyme like that, but you have to admit it's true. It's also true that summer with its green grass, Bermuda shorts and polo shirts would not be as much fun if it didn't come with memories of heavy coats, heavier boots, and landing on your tushie during your first encounter with black ice.

I pity my friends who are forced to live in places where a cold winter's day means you might want to turn down the air-conditioner at bedtime. Or, where the TV weatherman has nothing to do except report that the sun will be shining, and then say, "back to you, Jim."

I believe that deep in their hearts, most of them wish they lived where they would have a chance to experience real weather changes, and be able to grasp the concept of changing seasons.

I know that there are times when they wish it would cool off a bit so they wouldn't sweat so much while mowing the lawn under a scorching sun, or they could finish eating a double dip ice cream cone without it melting all over their new white shirt.

We are so lucky to live in a place that has four distinct seasons, and where during a normal winter, you can make a snow cone out of real snow, and a slushy describes a day when the temperature is above the freezing mark on the back yard thermometer for more than a couple hours. You tell me, which will give you the best bragging rights at a family reunion, tales of being able to cook an egg on the sidewalk or stories of tunneling through the snow to get to the BBQ grill so you can host a mid January cook out?

The Redhead doesn't share in my thoughts that winter is all about snow depth and double dipping temperatures. She hangs with what she thinks is the majority position of believing that snow belongs on the top of mountain peaks, and not on the road between out house and the mall, or in our yard. Well, maybe a little bit in the yard, but not on the sidewalk or driveway. Above all else, she believes that a person should be able to go outside without a coat, no matter what month it is.

I have tried to talk to her about layering but it's been hard for me to convince her that a necklace and matching earrings do not constitute one of the layers. I also seem to have trouble with the idea that sandals are no different than fur lined boots.

When I get ready to go anywhere, I am layered with a heavy jacket over a wool sweater over a heavy shirt over a turtleneck over a tee shirt. Sometimes I feel like that kid in the movie Christmas Story. I'm not going to shoot my eye out but if you push me over, I will never be able to get back up. Red gets dressed up in slacks, a nice top, and a light jacket. I am warm but can't move, she is warm and can. I don't understand!

What I can understand is that it's time to start thinking about making resolutions for the New Year. The first thing on my list is to wish everyone a very Happy New Year.

The second will be to embrace whatever the weather will bring, and hope it will bring lots of snow before the spring flowers start to blossom.

Fighting a Cold

It's only natural that just about everyone is obsessed with the loss of summer, the beginning of fall, and the sure and present prospect of shoveling roofs and snow mobile races. I know that I am guilty of beginning and ending almost all conversations I get in with comments about the changing colors of the trees. I think all of us have created our own list of happenings. It usually begins with comments about flying geese, shorter days, and complaints about not having all the yard work we promised to do last spring finished.

There is one thing that I seldom see on anyone's list describing the coming of fall, including my own. That is the first arrival of the dreaded rhinitis acuta catarrhalis. Ok, maybe not the first arrival because this nasty little critter lurks in the nightmares of children and day care providers all year long. We seem to notice it more after the trees loose their leaves, and schoolrooms fill to the brim with snotty noses and hacking coughs.

Schools are not the only places we can find evidence of the arrival of the rhinitis monster. It is showing up in movie theaters, shopping malls, and coffee shops all over the region. The monster is so small that you and I can't see it. You may not even be aware of its presence until three or four days after it has launched it's attack, and even then you're not going to know for sure where or when the invasion took place.

What you will know is that all of a sudden you have run out of Kleenex tissues and have developed a need to stand in line at the drug store looking for anything that will stop the sneezing.

With all the advances in medical knowledge and the proliferation of pills, powders and foul tasting liquid remedies available, it seems that something should make you feel better. If like me, you have invested more than a little time searching the hundreds of bottles and boxes in the cold section of the supermarket you have discovered two important things.

The first is that your eyes are stinging to bad to see, your head aches too bad to think, and there is no way of telling which bottle it going to make you feel better. The second is, if you are able to read the label, each and every one contains a suggestion that you get lots of rest, and drink plenty of liquids.

My thought is, if all these drug manufactures can't come to agreement on which potion is best, but can agree that getting lots of rest, drinking lots of water then waiting the five to seven days for the rino attack to be over is the best remedy, why spend the money?

So here I sit, four days into my seven day waiting period hoping that I can keep my nose dry at least until I finish whining about not feeling good, and can talk the Redhead into fixing me a big bowl of chicken soup.

Milestones

It is human nature to mark major events in our lives, like the first time we tied our shoes without help, the first time we kissed a girl, or even the first time we said "that" word out loud. Some important days don't require celebrations every year, but birthdays and anniversaries aren't in that category.

Yet, even birthdays are prioritized in order of importance. I like to call them called milestones. The first milestone we reach occurs exactly one year after we are born. When reached, we are no longer the cute little baby we used to be. We are a chubby little critter who is expected to be able to blow out the candle on the cake without help, then do something cute so Grandma can get a picture.

After the first one, the next three birthdays are dedicated to nothing more than getting the most presents from the most people while eating cake until we throw up. Then comes the next milestone, birthday number five.

At five years old, we think we are officially almost grown up. We get to spend most of the day with kids we never met before. It might be in pre-school, kindergarten, or some other institution of higher learning, but it is not at home.

Our tenth birthday has the potential of being a milestone for nothing more than it contains double digits, but they are not the digits we want. We want to be thirteen!

Thirteen is the magic age when we realize we are smarter, faster, and better than our parents. We are grown up enough not to need any stupid rules like doing homework or coming home before dark. At thirteen we know all about life and living, and we understand how ridiculous it is to study history. After all, it is nothing but stories about a bunch of dead people.

At sixteen we not only know everything of any importance, but we have a drivers license. Sixteen also brings the void that fills the nothingness until high school graduation and true independence.

Then we graduate and trade away our independence by joining the military or going to college.

Before long we get married and begin another series of anniversaries. We not only celebrate our own anniversaries but we have kids and recognize each milestone in their lives. Our life picks up speed and we face the fearful forties and the mid-life crisis of fifties. Then we face the depression of sixty and the shock of turning seventy, which is the point where we officially become old.

At seventy, you realize the people you thought listened to what you had to say were really listening to their iPods. At seventy, you begin to wonder if your children still resent the rules you raised them with and, if so, will it influence their choice of a care facility when the time comes. At seventy, people quit referring to how old you are and proudly proclaim you to be seventy years young.

Well, I don't want to get young. I worked hard to get old and have earned every wrinkle, every strand of grey hair, and both semi-working knees. I like my plastic teeth and being able to go to the movies in the middle of the day.

I even like the idea of paying less for meals in most restaurants, and having some kid younger than my socks asking me if I need help opening a door. I can hardly wait for the next milestone. I'll tell you how it is when I get there.

Size Matters
The Size of Band Aids

Most are aware I had a heart attack that required a band aid to cover the entry of the tool they used to insert some stents in to trouble areas to keep the old ticker running well. It seems heart surgery should deserve a huge bandage, lots of tape and hoses, and a definite slow movement when I walked. Not so.

I think I am a nice guy. I try to send a smile to strangers I see in the store. I keep to myself in the neighborhood and only plow snow or mow lawns when I am sure that no one is trying to sleep in late. I feed stray cats, cute little birds, and the occasional squirrel when the weather gets real nasty and I can't get outside to do anything else. Heck, I even watch my language so I don't offend anyone with my natural potty mouth.

I clean house, cook meals, do the laundry, and take out the trash before I'm told to. What's even worse, I like it. It simply makes me feel good to know that I am trying to do my share around the house with a smile on my face. So, why is it then, me being such a saint and all, that the dogs have made a game out biting me every morning?

I am usually the first one to get out of bed in the morning, and I like to release the hooligans from their crates before they start barking and wake up the redhead. I usually turn them loose before I put on my pants, socks and steel-toed shoes.

The bad comes when they see me and immediately attack my bare toes and legs causing me to skip, trip, and fall across the kitchen until I get close to the bedroom where Red is quietly snoozing away. That is the point where, out of self-preservation, my potty-mouth takes over and my good sense follows me into my place of refuge in the bathroom.

It felt good to be safely tucked away in a locked room. I could hear the dogs slamming their way through the pet door out of the garage for a run in the snow.

Before long, my feet were safely wrapped in wool socks, leather boots, and Teflon shin guards to protect my lower extremities. The demons dogs were busy chasing cats around the yard and I assumed Red was snoozing quietly in the back of the house so I fixed my breakfast of one poached egg, an English muffin, a piece of fruit and settled in to watch the old movie of the day on AMC.

Life is good. So good in fact that I failed to notice that the redhead was awake and sitting in her recliner next to mine.

This fact of life came to my attention when she asked where the pups were. I told her they were playing terrorist with the cats and she suggested I let them back inside the house.

I knew what was going to happen. I knew there was nothing I could do about it. I also knew the preparation is the key to survival.

I cautiously opened the door, jumped out of the way, and watched as the wet snow-covered dogs ran directly into the living room and jumped in Red's lap eager to help her greet the new day. Red had wrapped herself in a warm comfy blanket where she could laugh, love, and roughhouse a bit with them. I had run after them and in an honest attempt to be a hero, I reached for their collars to pull them away from her lap and the horrors of being licked to death.

And that, my friends, is why I keep a supply of band aids in the kitchen window...band aids larger than those I carry from heart surgery.

Veterans

As a nation, we have set one day apart from all the rest as a special day to remember and honor our military veterans. We cheer their accomplishments and sacrifices, and mourn their loss. We pat each other on the back and congratulate ourselves for our efforts toward making sure they know how much we truly appreciate their service. Then, we put on our everyday face and go about living the lives they co-signed for us.

My question to myself is: after their special day has moved past, and the flags and uniforms have carefully been put away, would I recognize a veteran who passed me on the street? And if I did, what would I say?

Most veterans I know, and I know quite a few, blend so well into the daily noise of normal living that it is difficult for us to see the pain of lost friends, missed holidays, and loneliness they have learned to accept as routine.

What do you say to the guy at the coffee shop who suddenly stops laughing at your lame jokes long enough to remember that he had heard it before from a friend who didn't come home? How do you react when this same guy quietly whispers that he was in Afghanistan when his first child was born?

I fully understand how difficult it can be for some of us to comprehend what it means to be a veteran. It's easy for us to look them in the eye and say, "thank you." We mean it when we say it, but do we truly understand what we are thanking them for. We may even be so touched by their service that we scrape up a tear or two without trying to understand what we are crying about.

In today's world, the phrase "welcome home," has taken on a special significance far greater than it ever has before. It isn't too late to welcome home those who answered the call to serve when our country was attacked at Pearl Harbor. There are still a few of them left.

It isn't too late to welcome home the veterans of Korea, who served when the nation was weary of war and desperately longed for normalcy. It isn't too late to welcome home the young men and women who came home to cat calls and derision after serving gallantly in Viet Nam.

And today, we have the special honor of welcoming home our protectors who have served and are serving in the war against terrorism in the Middle East.

I hope that without sounding too maudlin, I would like to offer my own thank you to all veterans, who ever you are, and where ever you served. I may not recognize you when I see you on the street, and I may never understand the sacrifices you made, but I honor your service and I welcome you home.

Call Me Great

For the most part, getting old is not a good thing. Granted, it's a lot better than the alternative, but we still like to moan and groan about the creaks and leaks of the aging process.

Our bodies don't bend anymore, gravity tends to cause sagging in places we don't want to sag, and we discover that the Lawrence Welk show isn't all that bad after all.

When we start reminiscing about what life was like when we were young, some kid will always remind us that he learned all about it in his history class at school, and if we want to drag main, we first have to find the Historic District of Old Town.

There are some good things I like about getting older. No one expects you to wear ironed shirts all the time. In fact, most of the time it doesn't matter if the shirt is even clean of not. It's kind of like when we were young and our date developed a run in her nylons. The first moment of panic passed quickly, then she pretended it just happened.

46

With time, spaghetti stains become the norm and not the exception.

I do miss having babies running around the house making a lot of noise and stuff. The banging breaking sounds followed by cries then giggles to me was always a reminder that someone just learned something new. Sure, maybe they were messy little things but so is life and they need to learn early on how to not take it so seriously.

As a young boy learning how to fish on the Warm River, I never imagined myself as a parent. Even when I was a twenty four year old sailor living in Sicily looking at the Redhead holding a brand new baby girl in her arms, I struggled with the thought of being a parent. Parents were old people who never had any fun. Then I found out how fun babies were, and being an old parent wasn't all that bad.

Of course babies become toddlers, become kindergarteners, become teenagers, and become evil creatures that turn your hair grey. Then before I knew what happened, the baby girl I first met while living in Sicily is holding a brand new baby girl of her own in her arms, and I struggled with the thought of being a grandpa. Grandpa's were old, smelled bad, and had spaghetti stains on their shirt.

When our first little girl came to the planet, I sent a telegram from Sicily to our parents in Idaho letting them know they had a new granddaughter.

When this daughter's first little girl came to the planet, I got a telephone call telling me that I was a grandpa.

This morning I received a text message letting me know that my baby girl's baby girl had a new baby girl of her own, and that makes me feel just GREAT!

Tomorrow morning the Redhead and I will be traveling to Salt Lake to meet her and I will be wearing a brand new shirt with a fresh spaghetti stain on the front.

All of a sudden, getting old isn't all that bad after all. In fact, it's absolutely perfect.

They have an APP for WHAT?

The Redhead and I were living in Catania, Sicily (Italy) when our first daughter was born. We had no mothers, aunts, or sisters to help us make the transition from freedom to parenthood. When the time came for us to leave the hospital, we were given a shopping list, in Italian, for baby stuff, an escort to the exit door and a kindly "good luck" from the hospital staff.

No how-to manual, no baby books, and no extra diapers. The concierge in the building we lived in was kind enough to take the shopping list to a baby store down the block and pick up the things we were going to need, and gave the Redhead a lesson on how to change a diaper. After that, it was pretty much "on the job training." We somehow survived, and so did the baby.

A month ago our baby's baby had a baby. She doesn't live around here so the Redhead and I had to go all the way down to Salt Lake to see them. During our drive we talked about our first daughter, and how our parents were not able to see her until she was a bit over a year old. By then, we were proficient parents who could change a diaper, heat a bottle, give the baby a bath, and watch television all at the same time. We were good.

We decided to share what we had learned about babies with our granddaughter and make her transition to motherhood a lot easier than what we lived through. Sure, she had her own mother, who actually had more experience with babies than Red and I did, but we believed it didn't matter because we were older and wiser. As it turns out, our granddaughter didn't need as much help from any of us as we anticipated. She had an APP!

Rachel is our granddaughter's name but I call her Ray. Besides, it's easer to spell than granddaughter. Anyway, we were at Ray's home playing with the baby when I heard a beeping noise coming from her cell phone. She came running down the stairs, picked up the phone and studied it like she was cramming for a final exam.

Then, she took the baby away from me, said it was time to feed her and disappeared into another room. The baby had been quiet and not making a fuss. She wasn't doing any of the stuff that would make a person think she was hungry.

Later in the day, we were watching the baby sleep when Rachel ran in, scooped up the baby and said the baby's diaper needed to be changed. I didn't smell anything so I asked how she knew. She answered, "I have an APP. It tells me everything there is to know about babies."

I don't know how in the world she synced the baby to the schedule application on her phone, but whatever works. I wish we didn't live so far apart. I'd like to hang around a while just to see how well the application works out for them in the long run.

Time to Outlaw Snow

Not wanting to seem like a troublemaker, I have been quiet about Yellowstone for most of the winter. But, I think the un-fair practice of nature in restricting old guys who have difficulty with tolerating cold weather and heavy snow from entering the park to watch the critters shiver should not be allowed.

It's not my fault that the winter isolation on the Yellowstone plateau that has endured for tens of thousands of years is one of the primary reasons it is so special today. I want my turn to drive along the Madison River until I can turn left, and find a spot where I, and the other old geezers, can sit quietly and watch the geysers do their thing. Special consideration is nothing new, and it shouldn't take any stretch of the imagination to come up with a solution to my problem.

Think of all the reserved parking spots surrounding any mall, supermarket, and hair salon in the country. Spaces have been reserved for handicapped parking, stork parking, employee of the month parking, and even special spaces for senior citizens parking. When I was a kid, they didn't exist, and all parking was controlled on a first come, first served basis. Then, someone recognized the need, laws were passed, and accommodations were made.

I don't see why this same sort of mindset can't be established for visits to Yellowstone. I don't know if the responsibility should fall on the three states that make up Yellowstone, or on the federal government that controls it. But, someone needs to make it illegal for snow to fall on the roads inside the park.

Maybe not all the roads, just those I want to drive over to get to where I want to go. To make myself clear, I'm not suggesting that all the roads in the park be kept plowed all winter, that's just not feasible. Even if it were, the snowplows would pile snow so high on the side of the road that it would be like driving through a tunnel and trying to see through the mountain to the other side. There is absolutely no fun in that.

A law was passed requiring a specific number of parking spaces be marked with a blue wheel chair and, zippo, people were going shopping that otherwise would have stayed home and let someone else shop for them. The freedom of movement, and the ability to get out of the house now and then was shared equally with everyone. And this was a good think.

Our government has the ability to pass laws that affect every aspect of our daily lives. It can tell us who our friends are, what kind of car to drive, where we build our houses, when we can go to the doctor, and why we should support the politician of their choice.

Why can't the government simply add an amendment to the spending bill of the day requiring that there be no snowfall on roads through the park? That way I wouldn't be held hostage all day watching Oprah with the Redhead.

In case you haven't figured it out yet, I want to go to Yellowstone, and I want to go now.

Nothing to Worry About

Can you believe that the sky was blue today? It was sort of blue yesterday, too. So that makes two days in a row. Well, maybe it wasn't blue all day both days, but the sun was as bright as ever. With the temperature reaching around 40 degrees some of the snow has started to go away, and I even found a little patch of muddy grass at the end of the sidewalk in front of the house.

I was talking with my brother Fearless, the beach bum who lives in southern California, and he was saying that he was worried about me starting to show signs of cabin fever and suggested that I pack a bag, grab the Redhead and come down for a visit.

If I said that I wasn't interested in sitting on the beach on a sunny day watching the sandpipers run up and down in front of the waves trying not to get their feet wet, I would be less than truthful. The fact is, I love the sea with her gently rolling waves, and her sweet smell of salt almost as much as I love the trees, mountains, and snow we have right here.

After our conversation, I started to give serious consideration to taking him up on his offer and planned to talk to the Redhead when I had the chance, and see if I could convince her that it would be a good idea. A couple days later, before I had said anything to Red, I got out of bed early and fixed a cup of microwave coffee, turned on the television to catch a bit of news, and learned more about earthquakes and tsunamis than I care to know.

I'm sure that you, like everyone else on the planet, have been following the story as much as I have; so there is no need to get into it here. Let's just say that our hearts, prayers, and good thoughts are going out to all the people in Japan who are affected by the disaster. I have a few friends who live there, and they have all made contact and are doing well. My friends in Guam and Hawaii are all okay, too.

Red finally woke up and made her way into the living room where I was watching the news. She stared at the television just long enough to hear that the tsunami produced by the earthquake was racing across the ocean at 500 miles per hour and was expected to hit California later in the day. Then she suggested that I call my brother to make sure they were okay.

After visualizing a huge wave coming over the top of the sand dune that separates Fearless from the Pacific Ocean, and the boats in the nearby marina all piling up on his porch, I thought it best to not say anything about taking a trip to California. As it turned out, the Tsunami hitting Southern California was pretty much of a non-event.

With the sun shining, the temperature getting warmer, and muddy grass starting to show up along the edge of the sidewalk, I no longer am in danger of catching cabin fever, and have no need to go anywhere.

We are so blessed to be able to live where we do. We are far away from hurricanes, tornados, tsunamis, and other less-than-nice things nature can throw at us. All we have to concern ourselves with are winter blizzards, summer thunderstorms, icy roads, and grey skies. How great it is to know that the only thing we have to worry about is living on the world's largest super volcano, and we play inside it all summer long. Life is good!

It Isn't Fair!

My hair is no longer brown, my vision is starting to fade, and I'm no longer able to leap over tall buildings or outrun speeding bullets. My skin is a bit saggy; my butt drags the ground and follows me around about three of four seconds behind. But with the exception of tonsils and teeth, I still have all my original parts, and most of them are still in workable condition. I have always felt that getting sick is a terrible waste of time, and constitutes an inconvenience for others, so I choose not to.

I may not have as much personal experience as most of my peers with doctors, hospitals, and strangers sticking needles into parts of my body that I don't care to discuss. But, I have spent more than my share of time reading stories in old magazines about movie stars, politicians and other dregs of society while waiting for the Redhead.

I'm not complaining, mind you; it isn't her fault that she has her own cup hanger in the emergency room, or that most of the local surgeons have tools named after her. I see it as part of my job to take care of her, go with her to appointments, and sit there quietly listening to her and her doctor discuss stuff I don't want to know about. My preference, of course, would be to keep myself as ignorant as possible about what happens after the nurse says, "please come with me, the doctor will be right with you."

Lobbies are quiet places well suited to reading, napping, and contemplating the real truth about why so much dust is bouncing through the shaft of light leaking past the half drawn curtains. No body wants to talk about why they are there, and the receptionist is much too busy staring at the numbers displayed on her computer screen to engage in snappy repartee.

I was told once that if you are prepared, you don't have to be bored while sitting around doing nothing. I carry a survival kit in my truck just incase I get lost, stuck, or the engine finally decides to quit working while I'm off by myself somewhere. It contains a couple blankets, a shovel, water, food, and a small butane powered stove to heat the coffee while I wait for search and rescue to come find me. It's not much, but it makes me feel better.

My survival kit for our not to infrequent doctor visits involves an iPod loaded with a bunch of old movies, a set of earphones, and a couple books. My favorite movie, and the one I watch the most while taking up space on a couch in waiting rooms, is the sci-fi classic, Forbidden Planet.

The best thing about this movie is that you don't have to know what's going on, and no matter where it starts you can watch a young Anne Francis walk around in a mini-skirt. Us old guys will know who she is, and why she rates an ogle; the youngsters are just going to have to "google."

Anyway, while deeply engrossed in the movie, I felt a sharp stab in the base of my neck, and heard a dis-embodied voice asking when I last got a pneumonia shot.

"Why me?" I thought. "Why is it that when I take the Redhead to the doctor, I end up getting the shot? It just ain't fair!

Life Lessons from a Redhead

John Lennon told us that life is what happens when we are busy doing other things. Life, in my alternate reality, is being married to a Redhead. Not any redhead, mind you, that redhead. I'm sure that somewhere out there, there must be a redhead whose tiny little nerve synapses located in her brain actually made a connection with normalcy. At least I hope so. I'm not trying to be mean or anything, and I certainly don't want to offend anyone, but sometimes things just are and there is nothing that can be done about it.

After we had been married for about a month or so, and I was released from the hospital where I had been treated for bleeding ulcers, I came to the realization that my Redhead might need a little help in the kitchen and offered to show her how to fix a pot of soup out of leftovers.

While I was busy chopping up carrots, celery, and onions for the stock, she was busy chopping me up for saying bad things about her cooking and denying that she had anything to do with my thirty days vacation in a hospital bed. Being a very smart man, and still a little weak from loss of blood, I kept my mouth shut and finished with the soup.

Supper was eaten in silence that evening. The only sounds exchanged between us were the slurpies that accompany a pot of soup as it disappears into places we don't want to discuss. At one point I tentatively glanced over toward where she was sitting and noticed that she was staring at an empty bowl. After thinking it over for a bit, I decided to take the high road and asked if she would like some more.

"A ho bo fo," she said.

I had no idea what she just said but assumed that because her command of bad words wasn't all that good, she must be making up her own, and I was in more trouble than I thought.

"Okay then, if you don't want any more I won't fix you any more."

"But I want some more." "I wanna ho bo fo."

I think that at that point one of her tiny little nerve synapses finally made a connection, and she realized she had a piece of celery caught in her teeth. She excused herself, disappeared for a couple minutes, and then returned with nothing stuck in her teeth, and a bit of toothpaste stuck in the corner of her mouth and exclaimed. "You need to get your hearing checked. I said I want a whole bowl full."

That was a very long time ago, and we both have grown up some. There are still incidents where I'm still not sure if her brain is wired right but that's okay because we suit each other. Life's lessons have taught us to appreciate each other's uniqueness.

Maybe that is why I wasn't the least bit surprised when she woke me up in the middle of the night last night screaming that her foot was caught in the oxygen hose she uses when her asthma kicks up and she couldn't get it free. But then, I'm not supposed to talk about that.

What Did Santa bring?

Being the youngest in the family, I had the responsibility of waking up early Christmas morning and checking to make sure that Santa had really been there. I was always surprised to see exactly what I wanted under the tree, but knew I would get in trouble if anyone else woke up and caught me peeking.

So, I sat quietly on the floor in the kitchen and listened for the sounds of someone else wanting to take an early peek. When I heard the slightest noise, I would whisper a warning to get back in bed at a volume loud enough to wake the neighbors and, of course, Mom and Pa.

After gifts were given and received, wrapping paper picked up and put in the trash, and a quick breakfast of oatmeal topped with apricot jam, I would start the phone tree calling my friends and comparing notes of the type, volume and size of the booty we had each received.

I remember one year when I got a chemistry set, telescope, and a new dictionary to show off. Not bad for a single haul! I can't say that I remember what any one else got, but I'm sure they were just as excited as I was.

For the next couple of days after Christmas, my friends and I would make courtesy calls to each other's home, and play with whatever toys had been left for them. Ball bats, board games, tinker toys, and a model airplane kit just didn't stand up well against my telescope or chemistry set. But, I never said anything because I knew it wouldn't be proper to gloat.

It would, however, be proper to gloat when we all were given permission to bring just one gift to school to show off to the other kids. I'm sure there were kids who said they forgot to bring anything when they actually didn't have anything to bring.

But there was nothing I could do about that, and I'm sure it would be worse for them if anyone said any thing, so we all pretended that they would bring them next time, and showed off our favorite gifts anyway.

Mine was a new dictionary that no one else had written in. When the laughing and giggling stopped, I came to understand that not every one was all that interested in words and quietly took my seat.

I think that as we grow older, we tend to forget how important it is to share the joy of the gifts we received and share in the excitement of others when they describe the perfect gift someone had given them.

I know I'm always excited when a friend shows up with a new sweater or tells me that her husband remembered to get her the book she had always wanted to read.

My favorite gifts this year included a color-coded, stackable, three-tier recycling bin, and a leather-bound edition of Merriam-Webster's Collegiate Dictionary of the English language.

I don't think I will take either of them to the coffee shop though. I'm not sure they would understand.

My Humble Apologies

The delegation of blame is at the foundation of most cultures around the world. Every day we watch a parade of politicians and sports heroes point their finger at anyone or anything except themselves to explain away the bad things they have done.

Republicans blame the Democrats for the failing economy, and Democrats blame the Republicans for just about everything else. Sports figures and movie stars blame an assortment of addictions for their involvement in a plethora of unacceptable behaviors, and the kid next door blames his little sister for the window he broke when he tried to hit her with a rock. After all, she could have ducked couldn't she?

It's not my fault that I didn't hear the Redhead talking to me from the other room. And, there is simply no excuse for her calling me on my cell phone to let me know I wasn't paying attention.

I can't explain why we are this way, we just are. You don't see a bunch of elk standing around blaming a high-powered rifle for hunters shooting at them, do you? And when was the last time you were forced to watch an interview with a fish on the evening news blaming rising health care costs for the hook stuck in his upper lip. It's time we took a stand and started taking responsibility for our own actions, and requiring others to do the same. It's not going to be easy, but then anything worthwhile seldom is. The Flip Wilson defense of "The devil made me do it," no longer works!

A week ago I looked out my living room window and saw grass. Not a lot, but the snow was receding around the edges of the yard, and the areas under the trees were completely bare. I was able to free my garden rake from a drift in the back yard, and clean up most of the crab apples out front that the waxwings had missed.

It was such a nice day that I even started raking up the leaves that I had missed last fall. While picking up the bits of trash that had blown in during the winter and had been covered with snow I decided to move my snow blower from the front of the house around to the back yard.

After running out what gas was left in the tank, disconnecting the spark plug, and a bunch of other stuff that needs to be done before I put it away until next winter, I went inside to take a nap.

Then it started to snow! Not only did it snow, it snowed a lot. The wind blew, the drifts started building up and there was a danger that the Redhead's Thunderbird would be trapped in the garage and she would be forced to stay home with me rather than go shopping with her friends.

It would be easy for me to delegate blame for the snow to the National Weather Service for allowing the snow to happen, or to Al Gore for inventing global climate change. It would be even easier for me to blame the Redhead for suggesting that I clean up the apples or the Obama administration for no reason at all. But I choose to place the blame directly where it belongs.

So, I offer all of you my deepest apologies, and humbly ask your forgiveness. The return to winter we are currently suffering is completely my fault. If I hadn't been in such a hurry to get rid on my snow blower, none on this would be happening.

Football?

To all my friends and family, I am not a bad guy just because I'm not a football fan. I may be a bad guy due to other things, but not that. So what if I don't know what is going on between the goal posts after the kick off; at least I know what a goal post is.

Like any other patriotic American, I napped quietly in front of the television last Sunday while my wife, bless her soul, yelled obscenities every time the wrong team made a point during the Super bowl. Kick the ball. Throw the ball. Catch the ball. Drop the ball; Steal the ball. What's the point? And, it's not even a real ball. Bowling balls, baseballs, basketballs, even tether balls are all round like a ball. This thing is pointy on both ends!

Try rolling that across the room to see if the dog will chase it.

I don't have problems with anyone who actually likes watching football games, even those who prefer to watch from the privacy of their own homes. I bet they would rather be playing the game, but fans are fans, and someone needs to watch or the whole thing would be pointless, and no one would make any money.

Even the Romans had their sporting events that took place in front of thousands of screaming fans. Of course, without the safety net of broadcast television, the Roman sports fans may have been screaming from fear that the lions might escape into the stands and have them for lunch instead of the other players. And, in the Roman games, there were no instant replays. Once you were eaten you were eaten, and that was it.

Speaking of making money, I have heard more discussion going on about the commercials shown during the Super Bowl than I have about the game itself. Even the news people seem to be fixated on the millions of dollars it took to produce a thirty second commercial, the millions of dollars it took to buy the spot to show it, and the millions of people who watched it during the game.

Common sense tells me that if that much money is being spent on advertising, there must be an expectation that more money is going to be made that way, than is going to be made by the game.

Put that with the fact that when the game is over, it's over. The commercials will live on forever. As an example, the conversation at the coffee shop went something like this: "Who won?" "They did!" "Did you see that cute little Darth Vader kid use the force to start his dad's

Volkswagen?" "I want one." "The kid or the car?" "The kid!" "I can use him and his force to start my truck on cold mornings." "Ha Ha Ha!"

I think that next year we should start a new event that will be bigger than any football game, or gladiatorial sword fight. I propose that once a year we have a worldwide celebration of television commercials, and during the break, show ball games. Makes sense to me! Of course, I probably won't be able to take a nap.

The Invitation

I received an email a couple weeks ago inviting me to attend my fifty-year high school class reunion being held in Pocatello. At first I couldn't believe that it has been that long since I set out on my own to change the world like the speaker at graduation said I would. But, after doing a quick reality check by looking in the bathroom mirror where all I saw was a grey haired old fat guy looking back at me, I was reminded that it had indeed been that long, and that I hadn't changed the world a bit.

I was also reminded that I couldn't remember a whole lot about high school except skipping class to shoot pool at Freddy's sporting good store, and marching in parades with the band. I was no more of a joiner then than I am now, preferring to watch what was going on around me rather than take the risk of participating. In my heart of hearts I knew that there must have been more to high school than that, so after rummaging around in the garage I found my old school annual and looked myself up in the index and found the list of clubs I belonged to.

The first listed was the photography club, after that came the...., well, there wasn't anything after that. It seems that photography was the only school sponsored outside activity I had any interest in.

I was too clumsy to play any sports, too shy to try my hand at drama, and my GPA didn't quite make me eligible for student government. I couldn't compete with the jocks for girls, had no interest in auto mechanics, and couldn't dance any better than I could hit the basket during gym class. It's no wonder I was surprised the find out that I had been invited to the reunion.

I don't remember exactly how many kids were in my graduating class, but I do know it was well into the hundreds, so I would bet that I wasn't the only one who got lost in the mass of humanity that was Poky High. With that many people around, most of us tended to travel with a small group of friends we had been running around with our lives.

My group of friends all lived within a couple blocks of each other and had been attending school together since the first grade. I run into a couple of them every once in a while and we always have a great time making up stories about school that we hoped everyone else had forgotten about. Mostly, we talk about how much we have changed over the years.

For myself, I don't think I have changed all that much. I still can't dunk a ball in a basket, I still can't fix a broken car, and I still can't dance. I do still carry a camera most of the time. Maybe my hair isn't brown and curly like it used to be, so what if my teeth are made out of plastic, and who cares if the six-pack above my belt has changed into a keg. I'm still the same person I was then.

I don't think I will be going to the reunion this fall. I mean, who wants to go all the way to Pocatello to hang out with a bunch of old guys whose names I can't remember when I can go to the coffee shop every morning and do the same thing?

Fallin Yellowstone

I don't think it is any big surprise to my friends or family that during the first week of November, the Redhead and I are going to find ourselves hiding out someplace in Yellowstone National Park. Hiding is a pretty good word to use, because during the last couple days before the Park closes to over the road traffic, there are just not that many cars driving around. The relatively few people that we do run into are mostly Park fanatics that show up for one more look before the snow comes.

It is a bit risky to go this time of year because you never know for sure what the weather can be. Even if the TV weather reporter promises that the sun will be shining and the temperature will be warm, it just isn't always so. However, unlike what has happened to us in the past, this year all three channels got it right. In fact, they got it more than right.

For the three days we were there, the sky was clear, the sun was shining, and we didn't see a bit of snow. I don't think we have ever had it so good. On summer trips through the Park, the sun is right overhead most of the day making most of the photos we take look a bit flat and shadowless. It is only early in the mornings and late evening that the colors brighten up, critters start moving around, and it's not too hot to get out of the air-conditioned car and set up the tripod.

Living as close to the Park as we do, the Redhead and I seldom miss an opportunity to make the short trip, regardless of what the weatherman has to say. There have been times when it was raining so hard we could barely make out the herd of bison lumbering along the centerline of road. But that never stopped Red from timing the shutter of her camera to click between flip-flaps of the windshield wipers.

Surprisingly, most of her rainy day pics shot through a wet, dirty window turned out pretty good. I think she does that just to irritate me, and all my expensive camera stuff.

With no crowds to contend with or the traffic they bring with them, it's possible to slow down in the fall and take the time to look at the scenery. And you can do it without the car behind you honking its horn letting you know that it is more important than an elk dozing off in a meadow and they are in too big of a hurry to waste any time looking at a mountain on the horizon.

Good grief people, that's why you came here in the first place!

Perfect weather; perfect sunshine; and no crowds of people to force you to hurry up when you don't want to; how could life get any better.

Well, it is even better to know that you can sleep late and not miss anything. You can drive to a pre-determined pull out, stop, and take as much time as you want doing nothing except watch the rocks in the canyon change colors as the sun moves across the sky. Then, be back at the motel in time to take a short nap before meeting friends for dinner.

The gate closed yesterday and, until it opens in the spring, I'll be organizing the photographs we have captured during the season. Damn, I love it here!

Scary Night

By my count, we are only a couple of months away from the most frightening two events of the entire year. But don't worry; I'm not talking about the first real snowfall that's probably going to come a lot sooner than you think. I'm talking about Halloween and the elections. Now that is really scary stuff.

Look around you; we are already seeing a major population explosion of spooks, goblins and, worst of all, zombies. The walking dead are all over the television, the papers, and occasionally right on my front porch. Zombie talking heads telling me how bad things are and threatening me with promises of doom and gloom if I don't follow the teachings of the great zombie of their choice.

If you listen closely to the moans and groans, you will come to understand that there is no hope for mankind because all the other zombies, which translates into any of the zombies, are at fault for any and everything you can think of that is bad for you and your neighbors.

The ghosts of politicians past are appearing on TV every day, singing praises from on high in support of a couple new goblins who want to take control of every aspect of your life and make you feel good about it.

It would seem that as often as we have to put up with the gnashing of teeth and the cries of despair we hear from our politicians and their cohorts on the evening news, we would learn not to be frightened. But frightened we are!

And, for those who are not frightened, maybe you should be. I, myself, have developed an irrational fear of red sport coats worn with jeans, and the words "special interest." I'm not sure why, but I bet there is a TV psychologist or radio talk show host out there somewhere who would love to cure me of my affliction.

It is okay though. Somewhere in my early childhood I was taught that if I am prepared, I would have no need to be afraid. I was also taught that it is possible to desensitize myself from foul odors by getting a job cleaning toilets.

In my case, I have started paying more attention to the political zombies ten-second infomercials than I normally would. By doing this, I have discovered that it doesn't really matter who I choose to support on Election Day, it is going to be wrong; and knowing that it is wrong, it doesn't matter what I do.

So what I am going to do is get ready for the other scary day of the year, Halloween.

At least on Halloween, the knock on the door isn't trying to take my money or my pride. The knock only wants me to part with a bit of candy, and in turn, I will receive a smile and a polite "thank you."

I wonder if the world would be a better place if underage pirates, purple dinosaurs, and beautiful princesses were to take over our government and the politicians be allowed out only one night a year.

Becoming Better

I don't believe in New Year resolutions, but I do believe in evaluating what I have been doing and finding ways to do it better. It is easy for me to get bogged down by details and, as a result, I have to determine a specific goal with timelines and strategies. So, after a lot of introspection and numerous charts, lists and cost v/benefit scenarios, I decided to structure myself towards improving my photography. I realized a long time ago I will never be a great photographer but I know I can be a better one.

I read an article in a magazine about why the photos we take on Sunday are always better than those we take on Saturday. It shouldn't make a difference but, if you take a critical look at your own photo library, you will find it is true. The writer explained how most of us pick a couple weekends a month for a photo outing. We take our cameras out of the bags where they have been stored for five days with nary a click, and we expect to perform like Ansell Adams the first time we peek through the viewfinder. By

Sunday we have had a full day of practice and, as a result, our photos are much better.

It has been said that taking a photo is a lot like shaving: if you don't do it every day, you get to look like a bum. I haven't shaved since 1976, but my hair and the number of photos I take have to be trimmed to keep me from looking like a bum starring in a TV reality show called, "Hoarders-The Digital Files."

Before the age of cameras with a built in computer, I would head out to Yellowstone with boxes of 36-frame color slide film. I took my time in figuring out the best composition and exposure for each photo, and even more time finding the best subject. When I got the slides back from the lab, I would carefully look at each one and keep only the very best of them.

Today, I carry my digital cameras, several lenses, three 8-gigabyte high-speed flash cards, and a half dozen or so that aren't so fast. With digital, I photograph everything I see, as fast as I can, with no limits on the number of photos I take. I keep everything, believing I can fix any of them on the computer later. The problem is, I can never find the good ones when I want to because they are hidden in the middle of thousands of bad ones.

I don't see myself going back to slides, but I can see myself not randomly clicking away at bison butts wandering across a meadow. I will take a few minutes for an in-camera review and use the delete button more often. When I get home,

I will review my day's work on a bigger screen and delete the rest of the not-so-goods before I download them to my photo editor.

I have a friend in Salt Lake who introduced me to a program called Project 365. The project requires you to budget enough time to capture the best image you can every day for 365 days.

So, there it is. His project has become my plan to become a better photographer. I will take at least one perfect photo a day for 365 days; then I will throw most of them away. It has worked so well for him he is considering growing a beard.

I just remembered another thing I heard somewhere. "Your reputation as a photographer doesn't rest in the number of photos you take; it rests on the quality of the photos you show people."

Hide and Seek

Already, summer is gone. Don't know what happened to it; it was here a couple days ago. Maybe it's hiding out with the Redhead's purse that she misplaced. It is probably somewhere within arms length of her chair. All I know is she can't find her purse, she wants it, and I want to find it for her.

I did find the switch on top of the electric space heater we keep in the living room. I think that because I am the first one to get out of bed in the mornings I should be able to turn it on and take the chill off the house before starting up my truck to head out to for my morning coffee.

Of course, it doesn't make much sense to run a heater in the front while Red has an air conditioner freezing in the back. OK, I'm probably not the brightest individual on the planet, but it make no sense to me that when the outside temperature gets down below forty degrees, there is really no need to waste all that electricity cooling down the bedroom just so Red can burrow underneath both of the down filled comforters she keeps on the bed year round.

Of course, I am smart enough not to complain, and it is nice to be all covered up and protected from the arctic blast blowing across the bed all night. Maybe it's just her way of preparing me for what's to come when the thermometer out back on the patio cracks from the cold.

One of my favorite things about the first part of fall and the beginning of winter is that I get to start wearing sweaters. Maybe not all of the time; yet, it still can get somewhat warm during the day. But mornings in a cold house are a special time. Especially when I'm the only one awake and there is no one around to remind me that I need to buy myself a couple new ones, because the old ones are old.

Just because some of my favorite sweaters might have a couple holes in them, doesn't mean that they can't keep me warm. And, because I usually buy them somewhat larger than I need, they seem to make my mid-section look a bit smaller.

I have a favorite sweater! It keeps me warm when it is a bit chilly, and it doesn't get me overheated when I forget to take it off when things start to warm up. Even I will admit that it's not the most fashionable sweater on the block, and Red has a firm rule that I don't wear it anywhere that people might see me in it.

When I break that rule, stuff gets real warm, and the sweater disappears. I have frequently found it stuffed behind the couch or buried deep in the back of the hall closet. Once I even found it in a box full of clothes that were going to be donated to charity. But, as you know, if you can't take care of yourself, you can't take care of anyone else. I decided to take care of myself and hid it where only I could find it.

This morning I had to search for my sweater. I found it under the table the Redhead keeps next to her recliner chair in the living room where anything she needs is within arms length.

The interesting thing about finding the sweater is it was right on top of her purse. I wonder how it got there.

I Need Glasses

When the Redhead and I were first married we had absolutely nothing. While setting up our first home in a housing project in Lexington Park, Maryland, affectionately referred to as "garbage gardens," we discovered that while the apartment came equipped with a stove and fridge, there was nothing to cook with or eat from.

Not being the type to become overwhelmed with the reality of survival, we went to the local discount store and came home with one pot, one frying pan, one popcorn popper, two knives, two forks, two spoons, two plates, two bowls, and two glasses. The bill came to an astounding two dollars, but life was good.

Two dollars might not seem like much by today's standards where numbers like millions, billions, and trillions are thrown around in casual conversation at the coffee shop without so much as a thought as to what they really mean. Two dollars was the difference between having a hamburger for supper, or pasta for a week. But, when you are young, none of this really matters.

What did matter was the need to insure that there was enough dish soap under the sink to wash both drinking glasses every time one of us got thirsty. I found out early on that no glass could be refilled, and that under no circumstances could one be shared. So, it was drink, wash, refill, drink, wash, refill. I think you get the picture!

Water and electricity were included in the rent, so using too much wasn't an issue. Soap on the other hand was! Going over the monthly budget, I discovered that purchasing a Dixie cup dispenser, and a large supply of Dixie cups was a whole lot cheaper than buying dish soap.

Without discussing it with Red, I went back to the discount store, and after saying goodbye to another two-dollar bill, I came home prepared to meet all of our drinking needs. Then I found out that water out of a paper cup didn't taste the same as water out of a glass.

The good news was, by me using the paper cups, more than once, I was able to cut the time and expense of washing glasses in half. But still, the paper cups didn't last all that long and I was quickly faced with the dilemma of not having enough drinking glasses, so I bought two more and two more until I reached a point of only needing to fill the sink with enough soapy water to wash glasses once a day, and life was still good.

Were older now, and don't need to struggle for survival like we did then. But even with all of the changes in our lives since the days of rationing dish soap, some things never change.

Like most people, I worry about how much water is running through the meter, and how much electricity I pull from the grid. I would like to think it's because of a concern for the environment and the need to reduce my personal carbon footprint. The reality is, I'm cheap and don't like to waste money.

A couple days ago, I loaded up the dishwasher after diner, and as I was pouring the soap in the dispenser I noticed that I was about to wash two plates, two bowls, two knives, two forks, two spoons, one pot, one frying pan, and half the glasses on the planet.

I also noticed that there was room left for another half dozen glasses, and a couple more plates. I'm not sure if I should run over to the local discount store and buy another Dixie cup dispenser, more glasses, or just bite the bullet and start the dishwasher.

Seven Things More Important Than Money

A couple days ago, the Redhead and I were talking about absolutely nothing when she suggested that I write something about the seven things more important than money. My first thoughts were about the three things that psychologists, motivational speakers, and itinerant street preachers have already identified as mankind's basic needs: "food, shelter and water."

Surely food would be at the top of the list. I tried driving my truck with no gas in the tank once, and during the long walk to the nearest gas station I had plenty of time to consider how much better off I would have been if I had remembered to bring along a sandwich, a candy bar, or something else to eat.

I got so hungry at one point I seriously considered eating the checkbook sticking out of my shirt pocket but even I knew that the most liberal application of salt and pepper or an entire bottle of ketchup could not make a piece of paper a meal, no matter how much money I had in the bank. However, when I arrived at the gas station one of the checks was traded for a hotdog, two snicker bars, a bottle of coke, and a gallon can of gas for the truck.

The lesson I learned from this excursion into reality was that neither me nor my pickup could function well without being fueled up once in a while. I also learned that food isn't free, and without some I could easily starve to death sitting in the cab of my truck while stopped on the side of the road.

Shelter from the stormsis the second thing more important than money. As far as shelter is concerned, I have always thought that if a person was well trained in survival skills had access to a minimal amount of camping gear, and didn't mind getting cold and wet once in a while, they could live anywhere.

Of course, I prefer sleeping on a bed with a thick mattress in an air conditioned motel room with cable TV over crawling into an army surplus sleeping bag spread out on top of a pile of rocks covered with ants. With nothing more than a debit card and an adequate account balance, I believe I could survive quite well on my own for a very long time.

Third, and last, on the list of seven things more important than money is water. I agree that we must have water. Without this simplest of all basic needs I would have no way of brewing a cup of warming beverage on a cold morning, and would be forced to hunt up a local coffee shop where all I had to do was drop a piece of plastic on the counter and a steaming cup of caffeine and four slices of bacon would appear from nowhere to give me all the fuel needed to survive until I got back home and fixed breakfast for the Redhead.

I'm not saying that having money in the bank will take care of all your needs. Actually, having a lot of money in the bank will serve no purpose whatsoever in a survival situation. However, with access to a checkbook, debit or credit card, and a boatload of cash you can hire someone else to survive for you while you sleep off the party you went to last night.

The remaining four things are probably a lot like your list would be: family, friends, good neighbors, and... well, let's start over and get this list prioritized.

Getting a Haircut

Much to the chagrin of the Redhead, I ain't no Robert Redford. No matter how hard you look, you're not going to find my face on the cover of GQ, and you will not see me posing for any swimsuit ads on television nor wearing a silk Armani suit when I go out for coffee in the mornings. But I do try to look my best whenever I can.

I shower regularly, brush my tooth every morning, and soak the rest of them in a cleaner every night. I try to keep as many food stains as I can off the front of my shirt, and have even been known to shine a shoe now and then. I think it's important for a man to do the best he can with what he has.

The one thing I do have going for me is hair. Sure, it's not brown anymore, but white isn't so bad. Compared to most of my friends it's still pretty thick, so I have no need to wear a ball cap to bed, or anywhere else for that matter. The down side to having a full head of hair is that I have to get it cut more often than I would care to.

Getting a haircut is not usually a big thing for most men, and it shouldn't be for me. However, sometime in the deep past of my genetic evolution a glitch in development occurred that resulted in my hair growing in un-natural patterns skipping from straight to curly for no discernable reason. To make matters worse, there is a "sweet spot" in length that, when passed by the hairdresser's scissors, causes my hair to stand at attention like the bristles on a scrub brush. Nothing can be done about it except applying copious amounts of lacquer and various gels to glue it all down until it starts to grow back.

Ever since I was very young, I have had issues in finding someone with the skills and patience to deal with my unruly fur. When I was still in grade school, Pa would just sit me down on a kitchen chair, get out the clippers and shear me like a sheep. When I entered Jr. High, I noticed that girls generally paid more attention to the guys who used a lot of oil on their heads to keep their hair shiny and slick, so I started letting mine grow out a bit, and that required going to the barber occasionally to keep it under control. That's also when the issues of getting a good haircut began.

It wasn't until after I retired from the Navy that I discovered my best chance of getting a decent haircut would be found in a beauty parlor and not a barbershop. Even then, it usually takes two or three haircuts before the stylist gets it right. When a proper match between my hair, a sharp pair of scissors, and a skilled haircutter evolves, I become a loyal and trusting customer. Of course there is a very fine line between loyalty and trust, and blindly going where you really don't want to go.

Last week, while sitting in the chair getting a haircut, the young lady doing my hair approached with an evil glint in her eyes and asked if I would like to try an experiment. Thinking that maybe she had found a new way to control my unruly cowlick, I said sure. The next thing I knew, we were talking about hair growing in places that I hadn't considered while she dipped a couple sticks in hot wax and stuck them in my ears. After a quick yank and a loud scream I realized that my cowlick wasn't all that important. Then she suggested that next time I come in, we do something about my nose hair.

I wonder if the Redhead will still keep me and my hairy nose if I were to grow a ponytail.

R U Pyng Attn?

I have come to the conclusion that the human brain has become no more useful than a water spigot that has been turned off. Its only function is to be there until someone opens it up so it can spew out whatever someone else has put in it and keep spewing until it's turned off again.

If you have any doubt about my hypothesis, try testing it by making a comparative analysis of the evening news and bumper stickers on the back of pickups at any coffee shop in the country.

What I have found is that the reporters on the news invest a whole lot of words in explaining a whole lot of nothing to a bunch of people who really don't care. Bumper stickers, on the other hand, use fewer words to say even less, but for some strange reason most people take these catchy phrases and use them to explain everything from politics to religion.

As an example, any one of the cable news programs can invest hours on having a bunch of news anchors sit around a table interviewing each other about the crisis of the day. It doesn't matter what it is; it only matters that they know more about it than anyone else. The pickups in the parking lot simply condense everything into a mind shattering display of simplicity with something like "Obama Sux." No need to explain it, or justify it; the sticker clearly says what some folks believe. Ta-da.

Of course, there are times when we have a need to know more than what someone else is telling us or maybe just to verify what they said. We could think about it for a bit, and maybe come to some kind of personal understanding of the issue at hand, or we could Google it. Actually Google works for me because I don't even have to know how to spell "flailing economy," Google will spell it for me, and then take a wild guess at what I really want to know based on my history of searches. Of course, all Google can do is refer me to a series of editorials written by a bunch of political pundits who got most of their information from Wikipedia. I guess that is okay; it's certainly no different than the kids explaining why they cheated on their history test. I mean, everybody does it.

In simpler terms, there is no longer a need to waste brain cells on remembering anything beyond whether I prefer ketchup and mustard on my hot dog. Or is it mustard and ketchup?

Slow Down, You Move Too Fast

Contrary to what my grandchildren might say, I am not getting old. I can still dress myself, tie my own sneakers, and chew my own food. Well, sometimes the chewing can be a little problematic, what with my plastic teeth and all.

There are a few things I used to do that are a bit more difficult than when I was a teenager. Sommersaults! They ain't going to happen.

It takes me a bit longer to get from one place to another, like from the kitchen to my chair in the living room, and long drives in the car require a lot more rest stops than they ever did.

The point I'm trying to make is that I can still do most things I did before; it simply takes me a bit longer to get it done.

I remember being a kid and getting my first drivers license. Looking forward to the freedom of movement and independence that comes with being a licensed driver, I studied hard, passed the test, and got a speeding ticket, all on the same day.

After years of driving experience, I learned it was quite a bit easer, and cheaper, to stay within the speed limit and not be required to listen to the same safety lecture from the nice officer and the judge.

In fact, I found that driving five or ten miles per hour under the posted speed will get you to where you are going just as well as any other speed.

Slow driving has a lot of other advantages over lost time in traffic court. Number one in my book is that it gives you time to look at something other than the centerline of the highway when driving over Targhee Pass on your way to Yellowstone.

You would be surprised at how many different kinds of birds are sitting on the fence line at the side of the road. And moose! By driving a bit slower than the accepted norm, you have the opportunity to see them hiding in the trees waiting for just the right car to run in front of. For some reason, they seem to prefer cars and trucks that are really zipping along to vehicles that are moving slower than they can graze through the fresh grass in a mountain meadow.

Driving slower does come with disadvantages; for instance, slow drivers seem to irritate drivers that are following close behind you on a two-lane road. Of course, their honking and flashing headlights tend to irritate me a bit too. Surely they know that the horn button on their steering wheel is in no way connected to the gas peddle on the floor of mine.

All that noise also seems to irritate the bison strolling quietly down the centerline of the Grand Loop road in Yellowstone between Madison Junction and Old Faithful. Just last week the Redhead and I were stuck in traffic behind a herd of bison who stopped right in the middle of the road to turn around and look at what was making all that racket.

Of course, the Redhead and I, not being in a hurry anyway, turned off the car motor, put the windows down, and had our lunch. The sandwich I was eating was so good I failed to notice that the bison had started to move again, but the car full of lovely young women behind us, who apparently were not aware of the benefits of moving slowly through the world, took it upon themselves to remind me.

The next time I go to the bookstore in Idaho Falls I have to pick up a new dictionary. I didn't recognize some of the words they were yelling at me and I intend to look them up just in case I hear them again.

I'm sure none of words they yelled at me had anything to do with the coyote that hunkered down next to the road watching me watch it while finishing up my lunch. We finished our lunch, started the car and drove off singing an old song: "Slow down, you move too fast..."

Privacy

I have been reading about, and listening to, a lot of news chatter lately warning about cell phone makers finding out where I am and what I'm doing at any given time. It seems they have installed some kind of program or application that calls them up every once in a while, and tells them whatever they want to know.

Apparently, at least one company even has the ability to find WI-FI locations that a complete stranger may drive past while talking on their phone. One article I read said that they can even see what you are looking at while on the Internet and borrow your passwords.

This new found knowledge of stuff going on in the real world got me thinking about all the COP shows I watch on TV. You can't hit the all purpose remotes on button without noticing that the detectives are looking at phone records, bank account access, credit/debit card transactions, and time spent in a highway rest stop. They can even find fingerprints and DNA on just about everything, and use it to arrest the bad guy within an hour, or just before the last commercial break.

There isn't even privacy allowed when you try to fly away to your favorite vacation destination just to get away from it all. Your ticket goes into a national database where you are checked to see if you're a terrorist or something. Then, when you check in at the airport, some stranger goes through all your stuff and plays with your underwear and everything. If you're real lucky, you can even get a naked glamour shot right through your jeans and t-shirt, then be felt up like a teenager in the back seat of a 1952 Packard.

Now, I don't know much about anything, but it seems to me that if I were to start following someone, keeping track of their every move, and taking racy photos on occasion, the judge would probably call it stalking. The other stuff would most likely be called assault. But, if you're a big corporation or the government, I guess it's okay.

Maybe the trick is to get rid of my cell phone, iPod, computers, laptops, credit/debit cards, check books, and any other trackable devices I may have and stop communicating with anyone. Then I can start doing all my business transactions, like paying bills and buying candy bars, cash only. Oops, I can't do cash only without a mailing address to get my checks or bank account for direct deposit, so I guess that won't work either. Also, with fingerprints, DNA and facial recognition software they will still know who I am, even if I'm living under a bridge somewhere.

I thought it might be safe if I were to find a way to transport myself back to the first century, but then I remembered how diligent the Romans were about taking a census and collecting taxes. A guy just can't win!

I can remember to do what Ma said, and make sure I'm wearing clean underwear before I leave the house. You never know who might see them.

Roadside Photography

It's just about that time of year for all of us roadside nature photographers to hit the pavement for another season of trying to capture that perfect image of any one of nature's last truly wild creatures.

Most of us are too old or lack the ambition to put on a backpack with a change of underwear, a few packages of dehydrated food, fifty pounds of camera gear and head into the wilderness for several weeks of peace and solitude. We prefer to find our wildlife grazing a few yards away from the comfort of our air-conditioned cars and XM3 radios.

With lunch as close as the cooler in the trunk and a thermos of steaming hot beverage in the front seat, we are prepared to park and wait for several minutes, if that's what it takes, for some unsuspecting critter to wander over to see what we are up to and maybe pose for a few clicks of our shutters before disappearing back into the trees.

The more adventurous sorts may even put several hundred miles on the odometer driving from one spot to another following the advice of others who saw a mountain goat grazing on the grass right on the edge of the road sometime last week. Who knows?

Maybe they aren't full yet and are still eating. I remember an incident several years ago when the Redhead and I photographed a black bear quietly biting the heads of yellow flowers in a meadow next to an authorized pullout just south of Mammoth Hot Springs in Yellowstone. That spot has become one of our favorite napping places on our trips to the park. Haven't seen a bear there since, but it might happen.

Having spent several years and thousands of miles driving the Grand Loop, I have developed a couple pretty good ideas of when and where I am more likely to be able to get a few good photos, and where I am not. The most obvious signs of animal activity are the herds of elk that gather along the river just before you get to Madison Junction, or the bison blocking the road while they meander down the centerline moving from one spot to another almost anywhere in the park.

In either case, you will almost be assured to get a good shot or two before a ranger kindly reminds you that you must get off the road and outside the white line before leaving your car.

Paying attention to traffic patterns while driving around is one of the surest ways to find animals within range of even a medium length telephoto lens. If traffic is flowing smoothly and at the speed limit, it's a pretty good bet that either there are no animals, or they are too far away to photograph anyway.

If traffic is stopped and people are getting out of their cars, grab your camera and join them. If you come on a pull out filled with cars and people are lined up with spotting scopes, they are probably looking at something a couple miles away, If they have big cameras set up on tripods, pull over and maybe you will get lucky.

If by chance you come around a curve and see a guy standing all alone next to a tripod and camera, and the Redhead sitting in the front seat of the car watching movies on her i-Pod, pull over and say hi. It's a good time to take a rest and I will tell you all about what a friend saw in this same spot yesterday.

Fishing with Fearless

Don't worry; this isn't going to be a story about the trials and tribulations of two good old boys trying to find their way to their favorite fishing hole. There are no bears, snakes, or scantily clad farm girls casting their own hooks. No thunderstorms, potholes, or broken down pickup trucks. It's nothing more than a story about two brothers standing on a riverbank casting for memories of growing up on the Warm River.

Way back in the late 1800s, our great-grandfather moved his family north from southern Idaho to what is now Fremont County. My grandfather was a young man who came of age, met a girl, married and raised a family in Marysville.

Pa catching his last fish. Warm River

From the stories Pa used to tell me, Grandpa's favorite fishing place was a small river hidden in a deep canyon a few miles from their home. During the summer he would frequently load his family in a wagon and go there for a day of fishing, hiking, and playing in the water. That is where Pa caught his first fish. Many years, and five sons later, that is where Pa caught his last fish.

With the coming of the railroad, and later cars, there was not much work in the area for a teamster so he moved the family moved to Pocatello. That is where Pa met a girl, married, and raised five sons.

I was the baby in the family, with Fearless coming in at number four. He is five years older than I and when we were little, that seemed like a lot. Now that we are both grey-haired old men, it doesn't seem like so much.

Neither does it seem to be that long ago when Pa would load us in the back of his old Chevy along with any of our older brothers who were available, and make the long, hot, all day drive to Warm River for a couple days of camping and fishing. It was on one of these trips that Fearless caught his first fish, and it's also where I caught mine.

There are a lot of "firsts" in our lives. The first time we drove a car on our own, the first time we discovered the glories of chocolate ice cream, and the first time our heart was broken by a pretty girl. One of the most memorable firsts for each of the five Marler boys was the thrill of catching his first fish. The ice cream will melt, an even prettier girl may come along, but that first fish can never be replaced.

Fearless lives on a beach in southern California now, and doesn't get the chance to do much fishing. Every couple of years or so, he will make the trip back to Idaho, and we get to have a couple more days fishing, and playing in the icy water of the Warm River.

It's changed a lot since we were kids sleeping under the stars on the riverbank. The tall grass, wooden outhouse, and log picnic pavilion have been replaced by well-groomed lawns, and paved parking spots for large motor homes.

What has not changed is sound of laughter from kids discovering the Warm River really isn't warm, and the squeals of delight from a child catching his first fish.

My brother and I didn't talk about it much, but considering time and age, I think we both wonder if each fish pulling on the end of our line is going to be our last.

There has been over a hundred years of Marler kids fishing the Warm River, and I believe with our kids, grandkids, and great-grandkids, there will be a hundred more. I want them to know why they are fishing there, and who fished there before them. I want them to know about Pa, his five sons, and the cold, clear waters of the greatest river on the planet.

The Perfect Day

Every once in a while we have all had one of those days that start out great and just get better with each tick of the clock, then something unexpected happens. I had one of those days last week.

There was nothing special about the day; in fact, it was really no different than any other day. I woke up rested, which in my world doesn't happen very often. It seems that I have been cursed with an internal clock that, no matter what time I go to sleep, wakes me up at precisely four-forty-six every morning. I know that no one should get out of bed that early unless they need extra time to get ready to leave on a trip or something, so I quietly watch the numbers on the bedside clock change until they read five o'clock.

The Redhead has her own clock that doesn't take effect until much later in the day. Even her dog doesn't begin to stir unless I pick her up and carry her into the living room where she curls up in a ball in front of the TV until I get dressed and take her outside for her morning business.

It is quiet at that time of the morning. The birds are still asleep and the neighbor's dog has nothing to bark about. No cars horns are honking, or doors slamming. Even the noise of trucks on the highway about a mile away seemed to be muffled by the silence of the stars sparkling in the moonless sky. I knew this day was going to be different.

There was nothing different about me entering the side door of the coffee house at Six o'clock like I do every morning. I sat on my usual stool at the counter and began checking the headlines in the paper like I do everyday, hoping to read all about the exciting things that were happening in the world. The most life changing event I found was a story about Paris Hilton being sued for thirty four million dollars because she wore the wrong hair extensions.

This is really going to be a great day I thought to myself while sipping on my coffee waiting for 7 o'clock to roll around so I could go back home.

About 9:00 a.m., the Redhead came out from the back of the house and I fixed breakfast for the both of us and let the dog out again. She settled down in her easy chair with her laptop balanced on her lap and disappeared into a world of MahJong while I napped through whatever babbling the Fox news blonds were so excited about. In my dreams I was thinking about how lucky I was to be living in such a perfect world.

Then I heard her call my name! "Dick, wake up and help me," she said.

She was sitting up in her chair, and had a distressed look on her face. The dog was pacing back and forth like she does just before a thunderstorm and I knew something was terribly wrong. "What can I do?" I asked. "Do I need to call 911?"

"No! Don't call an ambulance. Just pull my toe," she blurted.

Suddenly my perfect day became a nightmare-ish flash back to Pa, who towered over my four-year old frightened self, a look of distress on his face and said, "Pull my finger."

As it turns out, Red just had a little cramp in her big toe that needed to be straightened out. Pa's problem was somewhat more ominous.

On Being Prepared

Okay, it's been a bit chilly lately; so what! I am getting somewhat miffed at my friends and family from around the country who have turned a bit of chilly weather into a competition of who has it worse.

Sure, some of them may live in areas where they normally have to keep their lawn mowed all year long, and are now forced to use their back yard swimming pools as ice skating rinks. They knew winter was coming, and they knew weather patterns have been changing for the last several years, Why didn't they do something about it before it got cold?

One friend was complaining about sliding off the road, and had to wait for a tow truck to pull her out before she could hurry on to the supermarket; she had heard they were running out of eggs and milk. The weather channel had been warning her for a week that it was going to be bad, but still she did nothing to get ready. My heart goes out to her, and I wish there was something I could do to help, but it's a long way from here to Dallas.

There is an old saying that a lack of planning on your part does not constitute an emergency on mine. I sort of agree with that sentiment, but part of me feels a bit guilty for having a well-stocked pantry, lots of blankets, and an emergency source of heat ready if the power goes out. I know the roads are going to be slick so, if I really need to go somewhere, I keep a shovel, bag of kitty litter, a few power bars, extra blankets in the car at all times.

Oh yeah, I also try to keep the gas tank full, and have a six-pack of bottled water ready for me to grab on the way out of the house. I also keep a travel pack behind the back seat for the Redhead's dog, just in case.

This morning I got a note from a friend in Arizona who has taken refuge in an empty utility shed that has a wood stove and lots of blankets to keep them warm. He says they are doing well, and that they have a large supply of canned soups, stews and other stuff he can heat up on top of the stove so no one is going hungry and he says it's quite cozy. He even has a small generator that keeps the lights on, and his wi-fi working. There is a lot to say for being prepared.

Of course, most of us don't take time to worry about being prepared until we find out we're not. Like noticing that you're not wearing a seat belt just before the idiot behind you hits the gas pedal instead of the breaks. Or remembering that you should have bought more batteries for the flashlight right after the power went off.

But that's okay. I'm sure you're going to get a new snow shovel just as soon as you dig the car out of a snowdrift with the big spoon in the kitchen drawer.

Baffled

Once again I am a bit baffled. Not to say that I am any stranger to the condition, I mean, I have been married to the Redhead for over fifty years now and have been in constant state of bafflement since day one.

But this time, it is not her fault. At least I don't think it's her fault, but if I try hard enough I bet I can make it so. After all, I have had many years of practice in diverting blame towards her direction.

What has me baffled today is snow. Not the snow in and of itself, but the influence it has on the people who are walking around knee deep in it. All summer long they have been complaining about not being able to ride their snow machines into the backcountry, or fall off a perfectly good mountain with sticks tied to their feet.

Then, when a little bit of snow first hits the ground, they start complaining about the need to clear it off the roof of their house before it gets too deep, trying to get their cars out of the driveway, and of course, the cold.

When it gets cold, it snows. When it snows it's cold. That's the way it has been for millions of years, and I suspect it will remain that way for millions more. Unless, of course, you choose to live in Florida or on some exotic island in the South Pacific, you are going to have to accept it as a normal part of your life, not something to gripe about the first time it happens.

Be honest folks, how many of us looked out the window the other day and discovered the snow had moved from the top of Mt. Jefferson to the trees surrounding the house, and said a bad word. Myself, I got excited about it, and couldn't wait for the Redhead jump out of bed so I could show it to her.

This being a family newspaper, I am not at liberty to share her comments. Let's just say that all the snow within a hundred yards of the house mysteriously began to melt, and the dog ran and hid under the desk in the office. And so it was at our house.

I knew we were going to go up the mountain to see a friend who lives close to the 6,000 foot level, and I knew she was a bit apprehensive about the drive, and if the roads were going to be slick or whatever, and if the snow was going to be so deep her all-wheel Hyundai was going to be stuck and the snowplow people wouldn't find us until spring. I was worried hearing about it all the way up, and what was going to happen if she was right.

The highway was clear, not slick, and the snow plows were making sure they were going to stay that way. It was a beautiful drive through what looked like a Hallmark Christmas card. Then we turned down the lane that led to my friends cabin.

A half hour later, after a vigorous shovel powered cardio workout in knee-deep snow, the car was free and we continued on our way in total silence.

After a deafeningly quiet late lunch of grilled steak and baked potato, we said our goodbyes and white knuckled it past where I fell off the road and silently drove down the hill to our home in the valley.

So far there hasn't been a single conversation about selling the house and moving as far away from snow as we can get. Just random comments about tow trucks, bigger shovels and me being too old to be playing in the snow.

It's a bit baffling to say the least.

I Am Revolting

You can't turn on the television these days without watching videos about revolts and demonstrations in strange places all over the world. Faraway places like Egypt, Tunisia, Libya, and Wisconsin. Great masses of normal everyday people are marching in the streets carrying signs and banners, singing songs of protest, and chanting slogans from the bumper sticker of the day.

In some areas they are looking for freedom from despotic leaders or high food prices. In others, they are protesting the unfair treatment of government workers and schoolteachers' right to play hooky if they don't get their way. We even have government leaders, right here in the good old USA, who have runaway from home like spoiled children who didn't get the right toy for their birthday. And then, of course, there are the protesters who can't find anything else to protest against so they protest against the protesters.

With all this turmoil and discord moving across the planet and nothing of importance happening where I live, I am starting to feel a little left out. I believe that I have just as much right to be revolting as the next guy but I need a cause I can be revolting about. I want to walk around in circles with nothing to do except find a spot in front of a television camera for my sign or banner just like everyone else.

The other day I was looking out my living room window reviewing my core values in hopes of an epiphany that would reveal something I'm against, so I could complain to the heavens for deliverance from boredom. It was hard to think about anything important when all I could see was a big pile of snow. That's when it came to me: that instead of protesting against evil it would be much better to march in support of good.

Of course, it's a bit hard to find much good in not seeing grass or dirt for months on end, and trying to keep warm by running up the electric bill to record amounts. The only good I could think of was how much better off we would all be if we could get our elected officials to pass a law banning winter. Before we get all tied up in reality, I remember a story about a congressman somewhere that wanted to repeal the law of gravity. That's probably an unban legend, but it could be true.

What is true is a story I read in the newspaper a few days ago about a legislature in Montana that was proposing a bill declaring that Global Warming is good for the economy and should be supported. I have been looking for something to support, so why not that? After all, I have the right to be just as revolting as the next guy, don't I?

Now all I need is a couple thousand people to join me in coming up with appropriate bumper stickers with catchy slogans that we can print on cardboard signs to parade around in front of television cameras. We could also sing songs of praise to Al Gore, the inventor of global warming, and demand that our government require all snow be gone by Tuesday, and grass to be green by Wednesday.

It's true that I usually enjoy the winter months; however, raking the roof, using the snow blower, and hoisting shovels full of snow for several months makes me long for fishing gear, cameras, and sunshine.

This year is different; I am revolting against the grey winter days. I have had a snoot full of winter and I want Global Warming now.

On Getting Poked

I was poked today. I don't know why, I didn't do anything to anyone to deserve it. All I was doing was taking a bit of time off from my chores to look around in Facebook on my computer, and there it was. A poke!

In my younger days I would have know how to handle a poke. If it were a playful little poke in the ribs, I would poke back. Pokes became tickles; tickles became raucous laughter with pleas to quit, that were largely ignored. A poke in the nose usually required a somewhat different response.

I remember an incident from my younger, less civilized life. I was sitting quietly at the counter of a small café in Lisbon Portugal. I was minding my own business while sipping on a tall, cool glass of lemonade.

The quiet sounds of a guitar mingled with soft giggles coming from a dark booth in the back of the room. The quiet was occasionally interrupted by the loud laughter of false bravado from a group of under age sailors drinking beer at a too small table near the door. A big guy came in randomly cursing and yelling at anyone who was not him and poked me in the nose. I'm not sure, but I don't think his intent was to make me giggle.

I didn't want to make him giggle either so I poked him as hard as I could. The sailors at the table started poking each other. The guitar player ran for the door but was knocked down by someone running in from the street so they could poke someone, too. Chairs were flying, glass was breaking, and so many people came in from the outside that it was hard to find room to poke anyone.

But we kept on trying until the police showed up The poking stopped, the wounds were treated, a hat was passed to cover the damage to the establishment, the police left, and I went back to my lemonade still wondering why I was poked in the first place.

I still don't know what to do about the poke in Facebook. I guess I could poke back but I don't think it will make anyone giggle. I'm pretty sure it won't start a fight or have the computer police appear magically in my monitor blowing whistles and swinging clubs. I imagine that the National Security Agency will keep a record of who is poking whom but not much more than that.

I don't quite know to deal with this rapidly changing, electronic world we live in. What with all if its pokes, likes, dislikes, shares, friends you don't know and will never meet, and cute cat videos. I can see where it would be very easy to slip into a cocoon of ones and zeros and never be faced with the ramifications of a real world poke.

I, for one, refuse to be swallowed by the matrix. In order to reconnect with reality, I think I am going to ignore the Facebook poke I received this morning, sneak up on the Redhead, and poke her in the ribs.

Bet I get a real world reaction from her.

Another Big Bang?

For the past couple of weeks I have been bombarded with e-mails, text messages, Facebook notifications, and Google alerts warning me of the eminent eruption of the Yellowstone volcano. I have even received telephone calls from friends and family offering a place of refuge where the Redhead and I can hide during the catastrophic end of the world.

There have also been newspaper stories and television news programs from across the country, and as far away as England and Australia, trumpeting the coming end. My favorite warning came in the form of a video showing a herd of bison running for their lives, trying to escape from the park before the big explosion. I was talking with Smokey The Wild Cat and his friend Patches about the predicted event but they didn't seem to be very concerned. Of course, they are not very concerned about anything except insuring their food and water bowls are full and they have treats. Lots of treats!

Speaking of treats. If Yellowstone is in fact getting ready to blow up, Red and I have decided that we don't want to miss a thing. Sure, we could simply step out side, sit on the front lawn in comfortable folding chairs so we could watch the ash cloud climb into the blue sky and wait for the flow to turn us into instant crispy critters. But we would prefer to be a little closer so we can see the whole thing. I mean, you only get to see it once. We would like to see it from a little closer though. That's why we have made plans to be there when it happens.

The papers say that the event it eminent but they don't say when eminent actually is.

Thinking that someone should be able to make a decision, I have decided that it's going to happen somewhere between the 18th and 20th of April and will be operating out of Gardner for the weekend. I could be more precise than that, but I am planning on announcing my plans to run for the office of President that same weekend, and probably should leave a little bit of wiggle space just in case I change my mind.

Now that we are talking about minds, many of you may think I have lost mine. Well, I assure you that I have not. I have it right here in my pocket and can use it anytime I choose. Right now I choose to pull it out and put it on the back burner, so to speak, because sometimes a mind can be a terrible thing, especially if isn't used with great care and consideration.

I have learned the bison were not running away, but were running into the park so they would be there waiting for me. I have also learned that I have about as much of a chance of being elected president, as I have to witness the Yellowstone volcano eruption up close and personal.

We are still going to be there on opening weekend, and will be looking for you looking for us.

Zip It Up, Boys

I am told there are both good things and bad things that happen when we start getting a bit older. Wine improves with age as do most cheeses. Wines become mellower and cheese becomes somewhat sharper.

Tomatoes, on the other hand don't do well with aging process at all. I like to think that like a good wine, I have mellowed somewhat with age. When I was younger, I tended to get upset over almost everything. Now, no matter how bad things might seem on the surface, I figure what the heck, been there, done that and survived so why worry about it. Of course, like cheese, there are times when my attitude really gets to stink.

Then there is the tomato model, which I am reminded of every time I look in the mirror. One of the good things about getting older is that no one expects you to remember anything and when we do forget something we can just shrug it off with a simple "I hate this getting older stuff." Notice how I cleaned that up?

Another trick old guys can use to excuse inappropriate behaviors is to shift blame to the youngsters by reminding them that the time will come when they are old too, and we hope people will threat them better than they are treating you. Guilt actually works most of the time.

There are a lot of old jokes about getting old that I choose not to repeat here except to say that most of them have something to do with the proper use of a zipper. It's not that we lack the ability to make it go up like it's supposed to do. It's more like we just don't care anymore. And it's fun to watch strangers try to help us out without drawing attention to our obvious lack of social skills.

I have found that most zipper people come in three categories. The first is the over thirty bunch. They tend to try and ignore the situation by turning their backs after a quick glance, and then look over their shoulder to see if anything has changed. They will never, ever, under any circumstance do anything to correct the situation.

The next category is the twenty to thirty year olds. They seem to like to peek, snicker, peek again and then start with secret hand movements in an attempt to let you know the zipper is down without letting on that they noticed your predicament in the first place. Their gyrations ultimately bring more attention to themselves than they do to the position of my zipper.

The best group of all is the under twenty crowd, especially the real young ones. They haven't been contaminated by the social conventions of aging yet and seem to see things as they are and not how most of us think they should be. To them a down zipper is simply in the wrong place and they will tell you to pull it up. There are no embarrassed giggles or judgmental sneers. They see a problem, fix it, and get on with their day.

When I look at most of our current crop of politicians, who can't seem to see the world like it is and only see it as they would like it to be, I can't help but wonder what would happen if some youngsters were to walk up and tell them to pull up their zipper and fix things.

It needs to be done.

My Compass

When I was around seven or eight years old, one of my favorite places to go in Yellowstone Park was the souvenir shop at Old Faithful. I was fascinated with the giant log poles that held up the roof that covered the biggest front porch I had ever seen. Inside was a stone fireplace that reached all the way to the ceiling where I learned that it was not a good idea to look up the chimney when a fire was burning.

The shelves and racks in the store were chuck full of toy bears, coon skin caps, real Indian bows with rubber tipped arrows and fake cloth chaps that made me look just like an old-time cowboy. There was also a shelf filled with every kind of compass you could imagine.

There was one that you could like a ring and another that hung around your neck by a rawhide string, and one that seemed to have grown right inside a rock.

I didn't know much about compasses then, how they operated or how they allowed ships to travel around the world and end up exactly where they wanted to go. I didn't know why it was, that no matter how many times I turned it around, the red end of the arrow always pointed in the same direction. I did know they operated by magic, and I wanted one.

One night while we were watching the flames in the fire pit at the campgound, Pa reached into a pocket of his bib overalls, took out a small, round tin box and handed it to me. "Here son," he said. "Now you will always know where you are."

My brother Fearless, who was a Boy Scout and knew everything there was to know about everything there was to know about everything, tried to correct him by explaining that the purpose of a compass was to tell you which way to go if you were lost. Pa chuckled, stamped out the last embers of the fire mumbling something about never being lost if you know where you are.

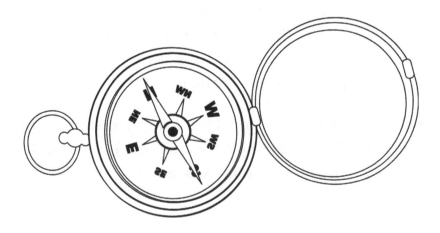

A few years ago we were having supper at Canyon after spending the day touring the new visitors center with friends. While we were eating, Elizabeth reached inside a sack sitting next to her, pulled out a small wrapped package, handed it to me, and wished me a "Merry Christmas" Then she told us all about the year it snowed in the middle of summer while they were in the Park. It was a tradition for them to celebrate Christmas in July ever since.

I will have to admit I was caught a little off guard by the gesture and could only offer a polite thank you while unwrapping the surprise gift.

The package contained a small oak box with a compass inside and the little red arrow was pointing directly at me.

A Salute to Liberty and Justice

A hundred and eighty some years ago our nation was engaged in war. Ships were being boarded on the high seas and sailors were being kidnapped by enemy forces. The capital building in Washington had been burned, the President and First Lady had been moved to an undisclosed location, and the city of Baltimore was under siege.

A young lawyer from Georgetown, a community of the outskirts of Washington City, was on board a British ship in Baltimore Harbor attempting to negotiate a prisoner exchange when the British fleet Commenced firing its bombardment on Fort McHenry. Not having the advantage of a live satellite feed covering the shock and awe attack, Francis Scott Key wrote a poem describing the battle on the back of a letter he had in his pocket.

If you were to read what he wrote at that time from perspective of what we watch on the television news, and not just as the words to a song, I think we can gain a better understanding of its real meaning.

Instead of the "rockets red glare" of Fourth of July fireworks display, I see the whoosh of a rocket-powered grenade streaking towards a passing humvee loaded with combat-ready Marines. In my imagination, the "bombs bursting in air" brings visions of two airliners crashing into the twin towers of the World Trade Center in New York City killing thousands of innocents, but not the spirit of a nation.

Like Mr. Key, I am amazed and relieved when the dawn's early light reveals that the flag is still there. Not flying from a flagpole at some tourist attraction in Maryland but on the shoulder of an American soldier in the Middle East.

The young men and women of our armed forces today are of the same breed as those who struggled through the night at Fort McHenry. They spring from the same seed that protected us from the tyranny of the Axis powers during World War II, and fought the spread of Communism in Korea and Viet Nam. They gave their lives on Omaha Beach and at Gettysburg. They died in Somalia, Lebanon, and on the decks of the USS Cole. They understand the concepts of "Duty, Honor, Country."

This Fourth of July, let's pay attention to the wanabee opera singer straining to hit the high notes during the opening ceremony at the city park, and hear the words, "may the heav'n rescued land Praise the Power that hath made and preserved us a nation."

Let's remember that we are One Nation under God who believes that Liberty and Justice is for everyone.

"O say, does the Star-Spangled banner yet wave, O'er the land of the free and the home of the brave?"

Happy St. Patrick's Day

Okay, as I understand it, St. Patrick converted all the Irish to the Roman Faith, turned the rivers green, invented beer, and chased all the snakes off the island. But he failed to do anything about the redheads.

The jury is still out as to whether or not the mass conversions he is credited with were really all that successful or not. The only green river I know about is the one that runs past Green River, Wyoming, and there are a lot of snakes crawling through the rocks there. I know; I saw many of them while hiking in the hills when I was spending summers with my oldest brother who lived there. Oh Ya! I forgot about the green river in Chicago. But I don't think it's really green all by itself. I think it gets a lot of help from used beer and green dye.

The color green seems to mean a lot to the Irish. Maybe even more so for the Irish who are not really Irish, but a bunch of foreigners who want to be Irish so they can have an excuse to celebrate St. Patrick's day, and help turn a bunch of rivers green. (If you know what I mean.)

As for myself, I have never had a lot experience with the color green. Well, maybe with the exception of a few green hotdogs and some less than good-looking green cheese. I have even sampled a can or two of green beer on occasion, which is never a good idea. And then there was that incident back in the 60s when some hot shot fighter pilot decided to see if I would like to experience the thrill of inverted flight. Even he turned a little green after experiencing my reaction.

What I have had some experience with is a redhead. Not just any redhead mind you, but a certified, certifiable, mostly Irish redhead with green eyes and a fiery red temper that comes with the package. It my own fault though, Pa warned me about redheads and I chose to ignore him. He said that if I looked a redhead directly in the eyes, she would suck out my soul and make me a slave forever.

So far his warning has proven to be right. That is, it hasn't been forever yet, so we will have to wait and see what happens next. But it has been well over sixty years so far; if you count the ten years I was her slave before we got married, and I don't see any chance of things changing from what they are any time soon.

So Happy St. Patrick's Day to all the Irish, real and imagined, with a special happy, happy, happy to my own favorite Redheaded Irish Princess whose eyes I am going to keep looking into, just in case.

Via Air Mail

Why is it that a guy who grew up thinking Via Air Mail on a letter was a really fast way to send someone a message go into a complete panic when his Internet connection quits working? And just when did handwriting classes evolve into the use of a keyboard and spell check?

I had a pen pal when I was a kid. Having a pen pal meant writing letters to someone you didn't know who lived on the other side of the world in a place you couldn't pronounce. My pen pal and I would share everyday experiences, tell about the things we liked and the things we didn't, and pretty much keep each other informed about every facet of our lives. You might think of it as being on Facebook with only one friend. The main difference is, with a pen pal all you needed was a thin sheet of paper, a pencil, a stamp and an airmail envelope. With Facebook you need a keyboard, a monitor, a computer, an Ethernet cord, a wireless router, a DSL modem, an Internet connection, and a couple hundred friends.

I have a few friends who still grumble and groan about the new world of instant communication. The Redhead and I like it, and frequently discuss what future technology might be introduced next. We update and stay connected! Not connected in a mob sort of way but connected with our computers, laptops, E-books, iPods, and smart phones.

When we were first married, I could be in the living room doing nothing while she was in the kitchen doing something, and we would yell back and forth to each other. That form of communication worked for us but I'm sure it irritated some of the neighbors.

With all the science fiction, technological stuff we have at our disposal today, we can now be in the same room together and quietly send text messages back and forth without irritating anyone. I have to admit Red can get a bit peckish when I send her a text, then interrupt what ever it is she's is doing to tell her to check her messages because I just sent her one.

Technology not only gave us computers and programs, but also brought us smart phones and opened a whole new way for me to tease Red. I wait until one of the news common-taters uses a seldom heard, antediluvian word hoping it will impress the listeners or make his silly comment sound smart. Then I ask Red what it was he said. She will stop what she is doing, find her phone and tap the app for Google to look it up. When she starts to tell me what it was, I give her a blank stare and ask what it is she is talking about. Points are scored on her level of response. I get one point for a disgusted look, and she gets ten points when I run for my life. It is, of course, all in fun.

The excitement of waiting for a letter from a pen pal on the other side of the world is long gone and the carefully written words have become outdated. We send LOL and OMG's. We communicate with lots of friends, many of whom we do not know, and we sign it with BFF XOXO. The new texting lingo and abbreviated language make me smile at the creativity. Still, I do miss reading the sincerely yours or the I love you, Daddy sentiments, and I miss folding the letter to fit in my shirt pocket where I can read it over and over.

Until the time when the old becomes new all over again, let me smile as I read your message and answer you with a ¤U2.

The King's Day Out

I woke up this morning with the air hose on my Cpac machine wrapped around my head like a kingly crown. Normally it's around my neck like a hangman's noose. The primary purpose of this relic from the inquisition is to keep me from snoring so the Redhead can get a little more sleep. Its other, more sinister responsibility is to keep me alert to the dangers of being smothered to death by the Hannibal Lector mask that I strap to my face just before bedtime.

This natural fear of death by strangulation got me to thinking about being where I am, and where I would rather be. Not that there is anything wrong with where I am, but sometimes I simply want to be somewhere else. Not forever mind you, I would settle for a day trip to just about anywhere. The hard part is picking a location that both of us would enjoy as long as it doesn't involve a dark theater, soggy popcorn, and plastic cups full of warm, flat sodas that invariably spill all over my lap.

The Redhead, seeing my kingly plastic crown, said that as long as it's Fathers Day, I could go anywhere and do any thing I wanted. Of course I wanted to go to Yellowstone but decided to surprise her by going somewhere else. After about two seconds of thought, I told her that all I wanted to do was get in the car and drive randomly around the other Yellowstone. You know where I mean. That part of Yellowstone that's not inside the boundary of the National Park but the part that right here in Fremont County.

After loading the car with snacks and drinks, I put my brain on autopilot, programmed it to Warm River and stepped on the gas.

Unfortunately, the car had its own autopilot programmed for the park so when we came to the turn in Ashton, it kept driving north. After finding a spot to turn around, I headed back the way I just came from and missed the turn again. Not to worry though, I convinced the Redhead that I had forgot to stop at the store and needed to pick up a loaf or two of bread to feed the fish at Warm River and Big Springs. I think adding Big Springs to our plan was a nice touch.

After insuring that the giant trout across the road from the old Warm River store, (yes I am that old), had gorged themselves on a high carbohydrate diet and fantasizing about being in the water with a fly line tipped with a white woolybugger, so we drove up the road to Mesa Falls. In my mind, Mesa is the most spectacular waterfall in Yellowstone country. The tall trees, green grass meadows, and bright yellow flowers lining the road are worth the trip.

While driving in around in what appeared to be a quite random manner, I convinced Red that by taking a short cut from Shotgun, over Stamp Meadows Road, we could get to the highway a lot faster. Red doesn't do bumpy, dusty dirt roads well, but I know she had a couple inhalers and a box of tissue with her so what the heck; it's only a mile or so. Why not?

After about six miles, lots of dust and bumps, a couple deer, and one elk later, we were back on the highway driving south towards home. The only thing that could make the day any better would be a nice dinner somewhere we had never been before. We found that at the new Mexican restaurant in Mack's Inn. It was a perfect day for a King.

I'll Do It Tomorrow

This morning the Redhead's dog and I were out in the backyard watching the sunrise and listening to the sand hill cranes bark in the distance. The guy who farms the field next to my property was running a combine back and forth harvesting the grain he planted last spring. Looking up, I spotted a lone goose passing by, apparently looking for his friends who were gathering out there somewhere.

Far to the north I could almost see the mountains peeking through the smoky haze that has been lingering around for the last month or so, and I was wearing a sweater. That is when I realized I had let another summer slip past me without doing all the things I was going to do tomorrow.

The problem with tomorrows is that they stack up really fast if you're not paying attention.

Tomorrow is a lot like a bathtub. You know it is there and you know what it's for but if you don't fill it with water, it's really not much use to anyone. The problem with a bathtub starts when you turn on the tap and the phone rings. Running water and telephones don't appear to have any kind of attachment and answering the ring is only going to take a second. But like tomorrows, the water is going to keep coming when you're doing something else, and if you don't pay close attention you're going to be cleaning up a bigger mess than you originally planned.

I'm not a young man anymore; I have seen a lot of tomorrows and have taken a lot of baths. From experience I have learned it is a good idea to have a water vacuum handy for those times I talk on the phone too long. I have also learned there is no tomorrow vac to clean up all the tomorrows that just kept coming when I wasn't paying attention.

I love it when the kid behind the counter taking all my money after I filled the gas tank on my pickup tells me to have a nice day. It is something they are programmed to say and it usually has no more meaning when than the obligatory "how are you doing" when greeting friends on the street.

But as I get older, I have come to appreciate the thought that someone wants me to have a nice day. In fact I frequently remind myself that I have fewer days in front of me than

I have behind and I refuse to waste any of them on a bad one. Not even tomorrow!

So what if the tub runs over. Think about how sparkling clean the floor is going to be after the water is all cleaned up. I don't care if the geese are getting ready to head south; my snow blower is filled with gas and ready to go. I even have new a new pair of gloves so my hands won't freeze. I may have put off fishing for too many tomorrows, but someone else is going to have a lot of fun catching the one I didn't.

There is a song that asks the question, "if tomorrow never comes?" My answer is, so what! I'm having too much fun today to worry about it, so I will do that tomorrow when I have more time.

I Bought a Weed Whacker

A couple weeks ago or so, my laptop departed the planet and went to live on a farm in Nebraska where there are lots of other laptops for it to romp and play with. It was a sad departure but something in my background training and experience prepared me to deal with it. What I wasn't prepared for was the loss of my weed whacker.

I have learned that the laptop wasn't really all that vital to my daily routine except to check e-mail while in the living room instead of getting up and walking to the office. I own an iPod Touch that gives me access to mail, Facebook, and as many games as I wouldn't care to play. It also is a great place to read books, something I didn't do with the laptop. The only real inconvenience of not having a laptop is not being able to watch old horror movies on hulu.com while pretending to watch chick flicks on Lifetime with the Redhead.

The weed whacker didn't do much except hang around in the garage waiting for me to take it outside and whack weeds. The last time I took it on an outing, it didn't want to do anything except sit there and make puttering noises when I pulled the starter rope. After checking the gas, changing the spark plug and pulling the rope a couple hundred times, I noticed the gas leaking out of the tank almost as fast as I could put it in. On closer inspection, I found that one of the fuel lines had rotted away so I attempted to replace it. Not being mechanically inclined, I should have known better and I shouldn't have been surprised when I broke something else. "Not to worry", I thought, I can always fall back to my back-up plan.

When the Redhead and I were living in Sardinia, I decided to clear away all the weeds and stuff from around the small villa we lived in and went to the local hardware store to get a weed whacker to make the job a little easier. My Italian wasn't any better than the clerk's English but with a little bit of pantomime and taking him outside to point at some weeds, he figured out what it was I wanted to do and sold me a scythe. You know, that big, two handled chopping thing that the grim reaper carries around on Halloween to scare small children. Well, I was out in the yard swinging this dangerous weapon around when the neighbor came running over yelling something about crazy Americans, took it away from me, and left a couple of goats to take care of the weeds.

I still have the scythe and it was my back up plan for clearing weeds and stuff from around the house we live in now. I sharpened it up and started swinging it around when the Redhead came hobbling out (she has a new knee and can't run very fast) yelling something about a crazy old man and made me put it away.

I have no plans of replacing my laptop as long as I can check my mail on the iPod. The scythe has been replaced by a brand new, gas powered, bright red weed whacker; and the scythe now lives on a farm in Nebraska where there are a lot of other scythes for it to play with and scare small children all year long.

Wee Wii

The Redhead and I work at the same place. In the mornings we leave home about the same time and drive the mile or so to our offices on the same road. I drive my ten-year-old pickup with the windows down and she rides in her maroon colored Hyundai with the heater going full blast.

About twice a week we go out to dinner at the same restaurant and sit in the same booth and eat the same things. I usually get there first, order for the both of us, and wait for her to show up.

After dinner she drives straight home and gets there in time to watch Wheel of Fortune on television and I drive straight to the grocery store and try to find stuff we will both like for supper the next day.

On weekends we like to ride to town together and go shopping at the mall. I usually drop her out at one of the clothing stores and then drive around until I can find a parking spot near the bookstore. The rule is, the first one finished with their shopping calls the other on their cell phone and then we meet over by the magazine racks and compare the contents of our respective shopping bags.

A week or so ago I was talking with my boss about my upcoming retirement when he asked if the Redhead was going to retire at the same time. His question kind of caught me off guard so the best answer I could offer was a shrug of my shoulders, admit that I didn't know and suggested that he should ask her and not me.

I explained to him that each of us has our own set of priorities and reasonability and that I learned early on that interfering with Red's priorities wasn't a real good idea.

The blank stare of the lack of understanding on his face led me to believe that any further attempt to make myself clear would be a waste of time so I smiled and walked away.

Later that evening I was talking with the Redhead about my conversation and she looked at me with "the look" and muttered the word "pitiful" and went back to her computer game.

I'm not sure whether or not she was saying that I was pitiful, or that the separation of powers that has kept our relationship going all these years was pitiful, or if my boss was pitiful. In either case, in a couple weeks we are going to start spending all day, everyday, together and I needed to find something that we could do together without going anywhere.

After a quick trip to Wal-Mart and back, I hooked our new Wii interactive game machine to the TV and challenged her to a game of baseball. It took a little coaxing on my part before she started swinging the Wii wand around the living room beating me three out of three games. Tennis and bowling had the same outcome so I decided not to try the boxing game that came with the set.

I'm still looking forward to spending all day, everyday together. And, I'm still glad I found something to do that we can both enjoy. I'm not sure what's going to happen if I finally beat her at something but I'm sure that it won't be that bad. After all, we Wii don't we?

Reading Stuff and Nonsense

I like to read. As a young pup, my most valued possession was my library card. I could go on about all the strange places, even stranger people, and the strangest animals on the planet that lay hidden between the binders of a book, but I won't.

Winnie the Poo and the adventures of the Hardy Boys were good stories but they didn't go anywhere. They were a lot like Lassie and Timmy. Lassie and Timmy go for a walk, Timmy falls into a well, Lassie goes for help. The only thing to learn from that was to stay away from dogs named Lassie. Everywhere that &%^* dog shows up, Timmy's life was in danger. No thanks!

I preferred the classics like Twelve Years before the Mast or any of the Leather Stocking Tales. Even as a young boy I thought that if was going to read a book, I might as well learn something from the effort.

James Fennimore Cooper, and R.H.Dana Jr. both taught me the importance of being truthful, and the power that comes from looking adversity straight in the eye while refusing to compromise your core principles. Of course, as a kid, I didn't really know what a core principal was but I think I knew what it meant.

Long before the movie came out, I had read, outlined, and had a notebook full of quotes and questions from T.E Laurence's Seven Pillars of Wisdom. Having made the effort then, I think I have a greater understanding of what is happening in the world today.

Now that I have finished with my feeble attempt at looking like some sort of an effete literary snob, I'm going to tell you that I am not. As the redhead and a couple of my childhood friends who happen to live in Island Park, will tell you, I was nothing more than a somewhat weird kid with a profound lack of social skills who didn't like to play baseball.

With all that, let's move forward into the real world of today. I started out the year with a list of re-reads. These are books that I have already read, but want to read again. I was walking myself through my umpteenth reading of Moby Dick when the redhead convinced me that I should be reading a more contemporary author.

I'm not going to give out a name because I might be accused of writing a book review, or even worse, a book report. Lets just say that it was a story about an inept game warden in Wyoming who habitually strayed outside his jurisdiction and had a penchant for wrecking pickup trucks. It was not a bad book. In fact it was pretty good. If I could, I would recommend it to anyone who asked. Then again, if I did I might be accused of plugging the book for commercial gain of some kind.

We all know that with anything good there comes the less than good, especially when dealing with an OCD personality trait. In this case, when I finished the book, the redhead told me the author had written another one. In fact, a quick Amazon search revealed that he had written a bazillion books and now I am duty-bound to read them all.

I remember the days when I would read maybe one contemporary novel every couple of years or so. Right now I am averaging one book a week and I am on book twelve. My eyes are red, my skin has taken on a grayish pallor, and I have lost five pounds. I will complete my mission. I will read them all.

With absolute resolve I was turning the last page of book twelve when the redhead came in and proclaimed that ## ### has another book coming out soon and wondered if I wanted to place an advance order.

Will someone please send me a Spanish/English dictionary, a fine print copy of Don Quixote, and a large bottle of eye drops? I need a relaxing break.

First Fish

I would suppose that most of us with connections to life in the caldera have fished the Warm River at least once. Myself, I have cast a fly into the river and caught a fish more that any other place I have visited.

Our family consists of at least six generations who not only waded in the icy water, but that's where they caught their first fish.

I would like to say that I remember well my first fish, but it happened before I was old enough to remember much of anything. If you think that can't be so, try to remember ever having your diaper changed.

Some where in the family archives there is a photo of Pa standing in the middle of the river right across from the old log pavilion. Stuffed safely in the bib of his coveralls, is me.

I used to wear the same kind of coveralls, the ones that had a bib with pockets to carry worms, grasshoppers, hooks, or anything else a person may need. They even had pockets for pencils but none for cell phones. Instead of belts, they had straps over your shoulders that made it easy for Pa to catch me should I fall and come drifting by.

I don't wear them any more; I gave them up when I entered the seventh grade. Strangely enough, I do have a childhood friend that still wears them. I don't know why, he just does. You may have seen him wandering around the caldera on occasion. If you do, wake him up and say hello.

Even if I don't remember my first fish, I remember fishing in overalls just like Pa. I remember hiking up stream along a trail on the opposite side of the river from the railroad tracks. I had hiked all the way to where a rockslide made it impossible to hike any further.

It was a nice day, but I knew if I were caught being where I was, it wouldn't be quite so nice after all. The rule was, I should never, ever, go anywhere beyond the small bridge at the upper end of the campground and the train trestle at the other end. That may seem a bit restrictive by today's standards but we have to remember, I was probably somewhere between seven or eight years old at the time.

The reason I broke the rules is all the fault of Pa and my brothers. Every night, just after sunset, they would come into the camp with creels full of fish. Big fish! Fish so big their tails would stick out the top of the basket. I wanted to catch fish like that and I knew the only way I could do it would be to go up stream as far as I could.

No one told me that when it started to get dark, the only way back was in the river. Another thing they didn't tell me was that there would be deep pockets of water that were way over my head.

Fortunately, Pa had taught me what to do if I found myself in that kind of predicament. He said that if my feet didn't reach the bottom, just stay on the top and point them down stream until they did reach and the river would pick me back up. Well, something did pick me up, and it wasn't the river.

It was dark and I fell. I don't know where those who rescued me came from, but all of a sudden I felt a tug on each of the straps on my coveralls and I was pulled out of the river and marched back to camp. After a stern discussion as to my stupidity, and lack of rule following, Pa asked if I had caught any fish and looked in my creel. My creel was full of fish. Big fish! Fish so big that their tails poked out of the top.

They weren't my first fish but they were definitely my best and they turned out to be the best tasting fish we had ever eaten.

Feeling Young Today

I was talking with a young lady the other day. I don't know how old she was, and really didn't care. However, if I had to guess, I would say that she was probably somewhere between eighteen and thirty. Maybe a bit older but I know better than to make a guess about that.

She works in a restaurant that the Redhead and I visit quite often and we had spent some time visiting with her before. She told us about where she was from, what it was like growing up, and all about her two children and how they liked to play outdoors and hated scary movies. We never discussed age so I was some what taken aback when she asked if I was old enough to qualify for the senior discount on our meal.

A person would think that with my white hair, beard to match, face full of wrinkles and scars, gnarly hands, and protruding mid section, it would be obvious that I am indeed a senior citizen. I could understand if she had questioned whether Red qualified or not. After all, she does look a lot younger than me and has been challenged about her senior citizen status on several occasions. Maybe it is her red hair or maybe it's because, along side of me, the contrast between our ages is clearly apparent.

Not apparent enough for this puppy though. She insisted that I tell her how old I really am. Being the gentleman I am and not wishing to cause a scene, I told her that I was really really old, and had been eating in this same restaurant before the world famous Teton mountains were just another flat spot on the face of the earth.

Not being swayed by my perky wit and sarcastic tone, she insisted that I tell her how many years that was. Buoyed by Red's steely glare and the smoke coming out of her eyes, I meekly told her that I had just celebrated my ninety-second year on the planet.

When the pain in my shins that was created by Red accidently bumping them under the table began to subside, I admitted that I was only in my seventies and sheepishly asked if that would qualify me for the discount.

This young whippersnapper started to giggle a little bit and when she regained her composure, she assured my that I did qualify and that she would happily deduct 10% from my bill.

She then started to give me the talk about only being as old as you feel and that I should start thinking of myself as being, "73 YEARS YOUNG." What a load of cr*p!

I am old and I am proud of it. I am proud of my thin, bruised skin that tends to leak whenever it takes a liking to do so. I am proud of the scars on my body that came from many years of clumsiness, not paying attention to the dangers of sharp knives, and the occasional bar fight. The baggy eyelids and sagging butt are the fault of Sir Newton, not mine. If it wasn't for his gravity, my knees would still work and my feet wouldn't be flat.

Getting old just means I move a little slower than I used to, take unexpected naps, but can still jump straight up in the air when Red asks, "Are you napping again?"

I've worked all my life getting old and now I am there, I plan to enjoy it for another seventy years. You say I won't live that long. Heck, why not? When I was a kid, I didn't think I'd live to be seventy-three.

It could happen, you know?

Caveman and Snow Flakes

I know it's an old story but it is just as valid today as it was a million years ago when our ancestors were still banging the rocks together trying to make a fire and get warm. I'm getting tired of shoveling snow.

I was outside this morning trying to remove some of the snow off the roof of my home and had a vision of a cave man wrapped up in a bear skin, squatting in front of a small fire. Upon close observation, I could see that he was trying to tie a big flat rock to the tip of a broken tree with strips of still bloody mammoth hide.

At first I didn't understand but I came to realize that he was trying to build the first snow shovel so he could push some of the cold wet snow that was blocking the front of his cave.

I didn't recognize the language he was speaking, but I think he was complaining about the shoddy workmanship of the guy who built the shovel in the first place. Then he remembered that he was that guy, and promising himself that if the d(%n rock broke again or the snow didn't stop falling, he was going to pack up his stuff, grab the first south bound dinosaur that passed his cave, and move to Florida.

I can relate to him, with the exception of moving to Florida. I have lived in Florida, and don't really care to go back. Sure, the weather is mostly nice. Usually it's not too hot, or too cold, and the beaches are always good. Even the occasional hurricane isn't all that bad. They don't happen as often as the TV news would like us to believe, and even then the wind blows real hard, there is a lot of rain, and then it stops. A lot of trees may have been knocked over, but they will grow back. Roofs may have been moved to Alabama but the insurance company will help build another one. Even the fishing gets better after a big blow.

A lot of my friends like to run away just before the first snow and go south so they can spend the winter on a desert sitting in the sun while swatting scorpions and chasing snakes all day. Sounds like fun to me, especially the snake part.

All we have to look forward to living here is more snow, more cold, and more isolation. Well, maybe ice fishing isn't all that bad of a pastime if you don't spend too much time thinking about it. I mean, who doesn't look forward to getting up real early in the morning and taking a hike on frozen water so you can sit on a metal bucket all day staring into a hole you cut in the ice? Then, you have to hope a fish might happen to swim by with nothing on its mind but whether or not to eat the worm dangling in front of him. The worm would enjoy the tasty snack unless, of course, the worm or snake is attached to a hook. Before swallowing the worm, he has to question if he would be the fish that would end up on the dinner plate of someone who is looking forward to a good fish dinner.

Somewhere in the fog of cave men, hurricanes, snakes and broken shovels, I heard the clear, sweet voice of the Redhead calling my name. She wanted to know if I was through playing in the snow and reminded me that we needed to get started on dinner so we wouldn't miss watching Blue Bloods when it came on television.

No more shoveling tonight. Maybe it will melt by morning.

Generation

Some time back my great grandfather left his farm in Franklin County Idaho and moved his family to the banks of the north fork of the Snake River, and settled an area they called Marysville.

I can only imagine the struggle he and his family had in starting a new life in a strange land. In my mind I can see him building a simple home, plowing long furrows in ground that had never been broken, and planting crops to sustain them through the winter, and shipping the excess south to help feed others.

I can't believe that he spent all his time and energy working. I can believe that he took time out for rest and relaxation fishing in the nearby rivers with his sons. Among these outings were trips to what became know as the Warm River.

There are many stories as to how the Warm River got its name. One describes the mist that rises from the water in the morning chill, giving the effect of steam lifting from the surface. Another is that it was a cruel joke, designed to get gullible young boys to go swimming in water so cold it could shrink them up into purple little prunes and make their teeth chatter so loud the birds would fly south believing that winter was coming soon. The truth is, it never freezes, no matter how cold the winter.

The Warm River isn't what you might call a mighty river. It's begins at a fresh water spring that shoots out of the side of the mountain full-grown, then flows a mere eight miles or so through a deep canyon until it joins another spring fed river called the Snake. It eventually makes it's way the Columbia River and ultimately pours into the Pacific Ocean where it carries ships all the way to Japan.

Pa used to tell us that if we peed in the river, the ocean would get deeper, and the ships would sail faster. I'm not sure if that was true or not, but Pa said it, so it must be.

Last week my brother Fearless, who lives on a beach in Southern California, came to visit. He brought along his granddaughter and his great-grandson so they could fish the same river our family has been fishing for generations.

His granddaughter is no stranger to the river; she has fished these same waters with her father since she was a little girl. Like the rest of the family, she keeps memories of this special place tucked away in her heart, and wanted to teach her son what she meant when she talked of coming home.

Fearless & his great-grandson-Warm River

I have to admit that I smiled inside when I listened to her tell stories of her father teaching her to fish and how his father taught him.

She told him stories of Pa and his five sons, and about how the clan had been fishing in the Warm River since almost before time.

And, how the river could be a healing place in times of sorrow and a place of joy filled with sounds of laughter coming from children catching their first fish.

Fearless and I watched the tip of the fishing pole his great grandson was holding bend and shake and saw the excitement in is his eyes when he lifted his first fish out of the water and place it on the grass. It was with pride that we watched his granddaughter teach her son how to carefully remove the hook from the fish's mouth and gently return it to the river.

I think we both quietly thanked our great grandfather for the seven generations of fishermen he brought to the river for a bit of rest and relaxation. Families really are forever when there is a river holding their memories.

My granddaughter & me-Warm River

I Will Not Panic

The economy is in the dumpster, banks are failing, crime is on the rise, wars are breaking out all over the world and Don Rickles won an Emmy. That would be enough to put anyone into a deep funky depression if it wasn't for the fact that we have seen it all before. Well, maybe not Mr. Warmth winning an award for being rude but that's something else again.

I can't speak for any one but myself, but I firmly believe that no matter what is happening around us, things have been worse, and they will get better, but only if we follow the words written by one of my favorite writer Douglas Adams and Don't Panic.

Maybe I have some kind of a quirky personality trait that puts me outside the bounds of a real world, but I just can't bring myself to fall prey to all the doom and gloom I watch on the evening news. Instead of getting caught up in the hysteria of political speeches, finger pointing, and the delegation of blame, I would rather see us come together and find ways to fix our problems instead of arguing about them.

That may sound a bit Polly Ann-ish to some and that's okay by me, I still think it can be done. Even Mr. Rickles was able to find a way to use rude comments, boorish behavior, and an outright nasty outlook to make us laugh at ourselves without hitting each other, and that's a good thing.

I will admit that there are times when even I can have difficulty coping with some of the stuff that is constantly bombarding my senses at every turn. I worry about rising prices of food like everyone else, and I wonder if we will ever be able to see the war in the Middle East come to an end.

But, more importantly, I worry about we are doing, not to ourselves, but to the planet we live on.

For thousands of years we have faced despotic rulers bent on placing their own greed above the needs of the people, and unscrupulous merchants whose only motivation is lining their own pockets with gold without consideration of the long term damage they are creating to meet short term goals. For thousands of years we have seen them come and go with the only constant being the environment we live in and the world we live on.

It's only in the last couple hundred years that we have been faced with the prospect that the damage we are doing to the earth may be irreversible. Of course, we can always turn our heads away and refuse to see what is happening to the planet, and go about our business of worrying and fretting about lesser things like what's going to happen on the next episode of our favorite soap opera.

Or we can do something more productive like finding out what the core beliefs of our next generation of leaders are and then take the time to not only vote, but to campaign in their behalf.

By becoming active participants in the world around us we can and will create a positive dialogue about the most important issues we are facing, and together find a way to make things better. The danger will come when we forget that we are all working towards the same goal of building a better society and protecting those things most precious to us. If that should happen, we will have no recourse other than to panic.

To avoid my personal panic, I constantly remind my self of the top three priorities of my own core values. They are life, the improvement of living, and a reason to live.

But that's a topic for another day. Right now I think the Redhead and I will go to Yellowstone and watch the elk work on creating their next generation.

I'd Like to Know

A few days ago I was in my living room, quietly sitting in my recliner pretending to watch news on television when something simply amazing happened. Buried deep in a barrage of stories about war, famine, political intrigue, double headed hurricanes and other pleasantly distracting stories of death, dying and destruction was a clip about a small restaurant somewhere that was giving a small discount to customers who prayed.

I don't do a whole lot of praying myself, other then giving thanks that the big truck that just cut me off in traffic didn't kill me or damage the Redhead's car. Okay, to be truthful, sometimes I pray that the big trout hiding behind the rock in the middle of the river is suffering from a deep depression and is looking for a chance to end it all just as my perfectly presented fly drifts over his head. That may be a bit selfish on my part but aren't most prayers?

I imagine that most of the prayers whispered in the restaurant are not asking for anything special. I think they are nothing more than a way to express gratitude for not having to go to bed hungry like so many in this world of ours do.

It would seem that the restraint owner didn't care about who or what his customers were praying to. He was simply happy to witness them unashamedly praying.

Pa used to tell us to celebrate the small victories because the big ones are much too rare to worry about, so for the next couple of days I felt pretty good about myself and about the human race. I mean, here we have two people doing something nice without looking for any kind of reward.

It's normal behavior when someone says, "thank you," to reply with an equally sincere "your welcome." In this world of self-centered "me-isms" we live in, it's big news when simple manners suddenly appear in a public place.

The experience can be so overwhelming to some, that they have great difficulty in understanding and try to hide their ignorance behind a façade of personal attacks. Just like two children playing a game...one wins, the other one looses. The looser doesn't want to admit his failure so he begins to shout, "you cheated, you cheated," as if that would make it all right.

A few days after I watched this news report, there was another one. This time it was about a group of atheists that didn't think it was right for anyone to shove religion in their face and threatened to sue. The news report didn't say whether any of them had ever been to that restaurant or had witnessed any prayers or discounts being exchanged. I'm left with a little confusion about the affair and have to question how anything can be shoved in your face when your face isn't in range.

I'm reminded of a story going around on Facebook about a little boy asking his father a question. I don't know where the story originated and for that I apologize. "Daddy," the boy asked, "if atheists don't believe in God, why do they get so upset when I pray to Him?"

I would kind of like to know myself.

Teenager in Yellowstone

My youngest granddaughter, Tylar, has been visiting us for a week or so. It's the first time we have been able to have her visit without parental or sibling supervision. It has been so long since the Redhead and I have had a teenager in the house, I had forgot how much attention they require.

Not that I mind. After all, it's her grandmother who schedules trips to the beauty shop for hair care, manicures, and toe painting. Being a good little grandpa, I looked at every piece of clothing she showed me after they got home and even made positive remarks about how good she is going to look in her new outfits when school starts next month. All I had to do was be there to drive the car and pay for dinner and a movie. Not much different than when Tylar's mother and Aunt Melissa were still living at home.

For me, the best part of the visit was taking her to Yellowstone. She had been there before but was too young to remember much about the trip so it was pretty much new to her. We only had one day and we left home a bit later than planned, so I couldn't take her everywhere I wanted. But we were able to go and that is what's important.

To a very large extent, the park was hot and crowded. Not many animals were dumb enough to stand around in the hot sun so tourists could take their pictures and it was much too hot to walk around the thermal features so we just drove around looking at the scenery. Of course, being thirteen, her favorite sights were located inside the gift shop at Old Faithful.

I loaned her one of my Nikons to use while we were at the Discovery Center in West Yellowstone and watched as she clicked away with her own Kodak Easy Share. When we got back to the car where the Redhead was taking care of the dog in the comfort of air-conditioning, Red showed me a text message she had received from our daughter in Utah.

It seems she had just received a photo of a wolf and wanted to know what we were doing to her daughter. Oh well! Mothers worry; it's part of their genetic makeup.

The battery on my camera died so the kiddo started using Red's. I wanted to share my vast knowledge of photography and show her what was important and how to frame the best composition. My mind flashed back to an earlier time when I tried to tell her mother anything, so I decided to stand back and let her do her own thing.

To me, the lens was pointing at anything and everything that had no real artistic value what so ever. Just snap clicks recording nothing much at all. I felt bad about her not being able to capture images of bears, bison, wild wolves, or anything else we go to see in Yellowstone. The surprise came when her photos were downloaded to the computer.

The screen filled with details of treetops, stumps of dead branches, wilted lily pads, and spider webs. There were colors! Deep blues and bright oranges glistening up from a couple hot pools, brown pinecones against the greens of the trees, a blurry cow elk dashing towards the safety of the forest, steam rising from geysers erupting on the horizon blazing white against the blue sky. They were all things I had given a pass hundreds of times in over a half century of trips to the park. We are going again in a couple days and I can hardly wait to see what she is going to show me next.

Her visit has been such a treat for us. She allowed us to look at the world and the park through her eyes. She taught us to, once again, enjoy the whole picture.

Thanks, Ty. You reminded me of the beauty that surrounds us, and you bring such joy to the world!

A Sign in the Woods

I saw a post on Facebook today, warning hunters, hikers, and snow mobile riders to watch out for falling deer. Underneath the warning was an explanation that leopards like to hide their kill in trees. There was no sign warning about leopards.

At first I thought it was kind of funny. I may even have given it a slight chuckle. I say I might have but I probably didn't. I spend way too much time watching cable news and have developed serious issues with chuckling, giggling, laughing, or any other outward display of jocularity. Pick a channel and all you will see is a bunch of real smart blonds with long legs sitting on a couch talking about a bunch of not so smart politicians who have a penchant for calling each other liars. Perhaps they are liars. I don't know for sure. But they are all running for the office of President of The United States of America and I hope that they are at least honest. Well, maybe not too honest; they are politicians after all.

For an individual to reach this level in the political structure, I would hope they would have developed the skills of creative truth telling to the point that truth and lies are indistinguishable from each other. Only then could anyone of them stand there and, with a straight face, promise to pay off the national debt, make a college education free to every one, re-build the military, create low cost health care, find jobs for all the homeless, fix the leaky pipes under my house and in the same breath promise lower taxes, increased wages for everybody who is not already a bazillionaire, and force an entirely different country to build a wall. Oops, I meant to say fence along their border to keep their people from running away from their local drug lords, poverty, unemployment, and corrupt officials. That way, we can deal with our own local drug lords, poverty and—well, I'll let you decide what should come next.

The reality is, we have to pick someone to lead the country. We know that whomever gets elected is going to be disliked by at least half of the people who elected him or her. The other half will want to see their leader raised to the level of sainthood.

As for me, come November I will vote for someone. That is what we do as Americans. Not because it is the patriotic thing to do, or even the best thing to do. We do it simply because we can.

While I am pondering my choice between a pathological liar or a megalomaniac, I will think about my own sign in the woods. It is the one that says: "Danger. Watch out for falling promises and lies."

Politicians like to hide them in piles of bull*&$#.

Signing out for now.

Happy Father's Day, Pa

My daughters grew up, became adults, and moved on to lives of their own. I'm retired and don't do any meaningful work. I spend my days puttering about in a back yard that others rarely see.

I mow the grass, pull the weeds and tend to a small vegetable garden, hoping it will actually produce a tomato or two this year. The grass grows back, the weeds get thicker, and the veggies just sit there doing nothing. The short growing season makes me wonder why I choose to live where I do.

On the rare occasion when I question why I live here, and Google Earth locks up keeping me from going anywhere more exotic than here, I drive over by the river and do nothing but watch the water and remember.

I think about where it comes out of the ground at Big Springs in Island Park to start its journey down stream. I imagine it greeting the water flowing out of Henry's Lake, and every other stream and river it passes until it meets up with the South Fork of the Snake after it escapes from Wyoming. Then, it travels on to the Columbia and ultimately to where it pours into the Pacific Ocean south of Seattle. In a vain attempt to teach me geography and acceptable social behaviors, Pa told me that if I peed in the river, people in Japan would have to swim in warm water. I thought, anything to help!

If it wasn't for the river, my grandparents would not have moved north in the late eighteen hundreds to establish a life at the base of Ashton Hill. Pa wouldn't have grown up in Marysville learning how to fish from his father. He would not have seen the need to bring me up from Pocatello to teach me how to cast a line, and then watch while I caught my rainbow.

When I left home as a teenager to join the Navy, I was often asked where I was from. I liked to tell people I came from a place that is upstream from everybody, where the river brings life to the sagebrush plains, and the fish jump right in the frying pan begging to be cooked for breakfast. I would tell them that if it wasn't for me and my contribution to the rivers flow, the Pacific Ocean would not be quite as deep nor as large, and the ships would have no place to sail. I would tell them I was conceived in the trees, born on a riverbank, and have caddis larva swimming in my veins.

If it wasn't for Pa bringing me to the river, I would not have learned the art of river gazing and the mind-cleansing impact of light sparkling off ripples below the big rock.

If it wasn't for Pa teaching me about the river, I wouldn't have moved here after retiring from the Navy and I wouldn't be pulling weeds in my back yard that is rarely seen by others, or waiting for the carrots in my garden to grow.

If Pa hadn't brought me to the river, I wouldn't be who I am. I wouldn't know the strength and peace gained from river gazing and remembering.

I hope he knows I like the way it all turned out and I really do like living here. Thank you, Pa. I miss you.

My Hobby

It's dark outside! It shouldn't come as any surprise to me because it has always been dark outside when I get up in the mornings. At least I consider it morning because it must be if I am through sleeping for the night.

For as long as I can remember I have been an early riser. If I had been raised on a farm, I think that my main job would have been to wake up the rooster and help him get ready to nag the sun into lighting the world for the day's activities.

I have tried to sleep in like the rest of the world, but it just doesn't work for me. No matter how late I go to bed at night, my eyes pop open a little after five a.m. I force myself to lie quietly until at least five-thirty and then sneak into the living room to watch infomercials or old movies on TV. I keep the sound turned low so as not to disturb the Redhead; although, I don't know why. She can sleep sounder than a hibernating bear.

For several years I would quietly leave the house about a quarter to six, and drive over to my favorite coffee shop to swap lies with friends over a cup of warming beverage. Around nine o'clock I would sneak back into the house without the Redhead knowing I was gone. I told you that she was a sound sleeper.

The coffee shop closed a few months ago. I think maybe the owners got tired of listening to the same stories over and over again, so they packed up one day and moved to Texas. Now I am reduced to heating up a cup of Maxwell House instant in the microwave and telling the stories to myself, which I admit is a bit boring because I, too, have heard them all, and I know how they are going to end.

I also know as soon as the Redhead emerges from the bedroom, we are going to have the same conversation we have had every morning for a bit over 50 years. It will begin with, "Why are you awake so early?"

My response will be, "Because I woke up." "Why did you wake up?"

"I was through sleeping."

Then I take the dog out for her morning routine, fix breakfast, and then pretend to nap during the morning news while waiting for her response. It is like lighting the fuse on a firecracker and watching it fizzle. I know it sounds a bit strange, but her quick and witty answers make us both laugh.

It is wonderful to start the day this way. It gets the brain engaged and active. She does have her secret weapon that warns me if I am dangerously close to taking it a step too far. You may not understand our morning ritual, but it has worked for us over fifty years.

Every man deserves a hobby, and she is mine.

Learning About Fishing "Wyatt"

It wasn't a dark and stormy night. In fact, it was a beautiful sunny day with no wind and blue skies. It was a perfect day to spend on the river fishing with the teenage son of a friend who comes up from Utah a couple times a year with his brothers and sister to visit their grandmother.

This kid is no ordinary teenager; he has a brain, a belt to hold up his pants, and can complete a sentence without a single use of the word "whatever." He even treats his six-year-old twin brothers like they were actually human, when some may think otherwise, and his sister like a queen. Which she is. Most importantly, he loves to fish.

Last year we fished together for the first time. After a few minutes at a local park practicing how to cast a fly line, we moved to the river where he was able to catch his first fish. In fact, he caught several more than I did, leaving me to wonder who was the teacher and who was the taught.

This year was no exception. When we arrived at Warm River, he was out of the car and in his waders, had tied on a new leader and fly, and was headed for the river before I got back from resting in the little room set aside for that activity. I think he wanted to fish and wasn't going to wait around for some old guy to get ready.

"You can't catch a fish unless you put hook in the water," he yelled over his shoulder while I was still trying to weave my line through the guides on my fly rod. I decided he didn't need anyone to teach him the finer points of fly fishing, being fourteen, all he needed was a driver.

I really wanted to be able to teach the kid something about fishing and decided the best way would be to wait for him to approach me for help in untangling a line, picking out a wind knot, or removing a hook from his ear. Anything would do.

I have a nephew who is working as a camp host so I hooked up with him for a bit in the parking lot, and visited for a while hoping that the kid would come looking for me, so I could share some of my great wisdom in front of a witness, but it didn't happen.

My nephew, George, went back to work, and I wandered over to the river, arriving just in time to watch the kid carefully release what I presumed to be "another fish" back into the water. "How many did you catch?" he yelled from the middle of the river.

Now was my opportunity to teach him the most important lesson a real fisherman needs to learn. I was going to teach him how to lie.

"I didn't keep count," I yelled over the rush of the river.

"Hard to do in the parking lot," he yelled back.

"Just wait until next time, Wyatt!" "Yeah," I said to myself. "Just wait."

Thank You

Thanksgiving is a day to give thanks. Sounds kind of silly when you put it that way, but what better way is there? Even the hardest of hearts can find something to be thankful for at least once a year. The rest of us can be thankful every day when we remember to wake up, and every night for having such a good day.

I'm going to try and tell a story about a guy. He is no one special, just a guy who likes people, sunshine, and puppies. He is not a movie star, a war hero, a powerful railroad magnate, or politician with a self imposed mission to save us from ourselves. His great pleasure is moving through life doing the best he can with what he has, while trying not to be a bother to anyone. He simply likes who he is, and likes to see people smile.

He got lucky! A beautiful young lady said that she would like to go with him wherever he went. She wanted to talk with strangers, eat weird food, learn new languages, and maybe create a couple of little girls along the way.

You see, this guy was born to a military way of life. His grandfather and great uncle joined the Army and went to the Philippines' during the Spanish American War. When this guy was very young, he would stand at attention near the base of Grandpa's flag, and along with his four brothers, salute while Gramps played "Taps" on his trombone. Grandpa said it would help us remember the men who were dying in some far away war being fought so we could be free.

His mother had five sons. When the time came, each of them left home to join the military.

The eldest son, Marvin, joined the Navy and fought the Japanese in the South Pacific during World War II.

The number two son, Norman, joined the Army and went to Germany as a combat medic.

The middle son, Carl, joined the Navy like his oldest brother, and saw service during the Korean War, and thirty years later he retired from the Naval Reserve as a Captain.

His other brother, Frank, number four on the list, went into the Navy and retired after twenty-plus years service as a Chief Petty Officer. During this time, he served two tours of duty in Viet Nam.

The last one on the list, the one married to the Redhead, retired from the Navy after twenty-years six-months total service. The mother bragged about having at least one son in the military from 1943 to 1981.

Last week, the Redhead and I went up to Island Park for the Friends of the Island Park Library annual Christmas party. We had a great time, ate great food, and visited with a lot of new friends.

Towards the end of the party, the speaker told a story about the women in Island Park who had been making quilts for those who had served in the military. This year they decided to present quilts to veterans who lived in or had connections with Island Park.

She started to call out the names of those who were going to receive quilts, and guess what?

The first name called was this guy, me, the guy who likes sunshine and puppies. The guy whose four brothers and grandfather had fought in four different wars.

I don't cry! It's just not something we did in our family. However, I will admit that I choked up a bit and had a small allergic reaction that filled my eyes with water. Not from being presented with a quilt. But from the realization that someone noticed who we were and what we did, and they remembered.

Thank you.

Halloween Costumes

Halloween brings to mind thoughts of evil creatures rising from misty graves and attacking innocent villagers and having them for lunch. Or man made monsters cobbled together from bodies stolen from cemeteries right after their first owners were executed by being hung or beheaded for committing the most horrendous of crimes. And the most horrible monsters of all, purple dinosaurs, that come banging on you door demanding candy.

This, the most frightening time of the year, got me to thinking about red hair and why this simple genetic mutation causes otherwise sweet normal human beings to act in a less than normal manner. In an attempt to find an answer to this unsolvable question, I went to that vast repository of knowledge called the Internet.

I wasn't looking for the common garden variety of redhead; I was looking for the select few from history that would shed a little light on why redheads are saddled with a reputation that maybe they don't really deserve.

The earliest reference I could find goes all the way back to the Stone Age where, according to one study I found, DNA testing has shown that at least one Neanderthal woman had red hair. I couldn't help but ask myself if hair pigment had anything to do with them not being around anymore.

I was more than a little surprised to find out that after Wilma the Neanderthal brought their species to an end, another Redhead named Cleopatra, who like all redheads, must have been a real hottie.

More pertinent to my personal research into the red headed mindset comes from a Celtic queen named Boudicca who in 60 AD, to fill a revenge need after the murder of her husband and the rape of her daughters and herself, formed an army and waged an attempt to kick the Romans out of Britton. Legend has it that, prior to going into battle, she would take off her top just to let her enemies know it was a woman who was whipping them.

Boudicca's attempt failed but an earlier queen had sent the entire Roman Empire into state of civil war after wooing two of their greatest generals and eventually brought an end the republic, which was replaced by a series of ruthless emperors. Whether or not it was Cleopatra's red hair that did the damage is open to argument, but we seem to have a trend that explains the Redhead's penchant for being an in-charge sort of person. But then, there is more to the Redhead personality than being strong and independent; they also have a tendency to be just a little bit ditsy.

Which brings up the third most famous Redhead in history. Lucy! I don't mean the proto-human Lucy that recently went on exhibition across the country; I'm talking about Lucile Ball's character on the television show "I Love Lucy." Who can ever forget her getting drunk stomping grapes or shoveling chocolates into her mouth as fast as she can? A definite personality trait shared by all redheads.

So there you have it kids, the scariest costume for this Halloween is nothing more than a red wig and an attitude. You get to choose whether of not you want to be in charge like Boudicca, a charmer like Cleopatra, or a ditz like Lucy.

If you want to be really scary, try bringing in a little bit of each. That way nobody will ever figure you out.

Insanity

Albert Einstein described insanity as "doing the same thing over and over again expecting different results." That may be true in some circles but I don't think it accurately describes my life. I have been known to frequently do many of the same things I have done before and fully expect the results to be the same each time but they seldom are.

A simple example could be using a less than appropriate, but completely accurate, adjective to describe the actions of a driver who cuts me off in traffic on an icy road. We already know he is an idiot and exclaiming to the world what kind of idiot he is may be a bit of overkill and will certainly precipitate a response.

It would seem the normal response expected would involve, at best, a broken nose and, at worst, an overnight stay in the emergency room. It could be assumed the response would not change from idiot to idiot. Einstein's belief that I would get a broken nose every time I called some one a special kind of idiot would keep me from doing it unless I had previously experienced when the behavior elicited a smile and a wave.

The distance from my house to Old Faithful in Yellowstone National Park is only 54.4 miles. The maximum speed a crow flies is 30 miles per hour which if I were able to fly as a crow flies, I could be at Old Faithful in no time at all. It takes a lot longer when I use roads and such but I still don't stand in my back yard flapping my arms in an attempt to get airborne. I know from experience that is not going to work and to keep trying would be insane.

However, I believe it isn't insane to stand in the same backyard looking east and a bit to the north and believe I can actually see the steam rise up from the horizon with each eruption.

On a quiet night, if I listen real close, I think I can hear the grunting of bison walking the centerline on the road along the Madison River and the bawling of the newborn calves.

I can envision the morning light creeping over the mountains, slowly bringing light to the valley floor along the Lamar

River, revealing herds of elk, bison, and an occasional peek at a lone badger waddling through the grass.

I know there are some who may question the sanity of someone, who by closing his eyes, can see the whiteness of the terraces at Mammoth Hot Springs or mist rising up from waterfalls plunging over the yellow walls of the Grand Canyon of Yellowstone.

What I love best about Yellowstone is the ever-changing sameness. The knowledge that Yellowstone country has been here for thousands of years and knowing it will be here for thousands more gives comfort and stability to the insanity of our world. It is also a whole lot better than a broken nose.

Preserve and Protect

Once upon a time there was a fisherman who told everyone that he was the greatest fisherman that ever was. Every day he would arm himself with his favorite fly rod, a box full of flies, a pair of designer waders and his very expensive custom made boots with the non-slip soles and head for the closest river.

Every day he would return home with a stringer full of fish, and stories about the giant rainbow trout that lived under a rock in the deepest part of the river that he was going to catch someday. No one dared question his skills at finding fish in the shallowest stream, nor his ability to quickly bring them to the communal frying pan. The consistency of success cannot be argued against.

One day, after performing his morning ritual of attaching a new specially tapered leader to the end of his line, and insuring that all of the flies were arranged by size, entomological category, frequency of use and how pretty they are, he waved goodbye the to lesser beings and went fishing.

All day long he presented his flies to the slightest disturbance in the waters surface indicating a feeding fish, and nothing happened. He systematically tried every fly in his arsenal with no results. In sheer frustration, he put away his collection of dry flies. Looking around to make sure no one was watching, he dug deep into the secret pocket of his fishing vest and found his stash of "secret weapons." Nymphs!

These bulky, heavy, buggy looking bugs were designed to bounce along the bottom of the river in hopes of hitting a trout smack on the snout, tricking them into feeding when they weren't hungry. This was his last chance of bringing home at least some fish to prove how great a fisherman he was.

As the sun set in the western sky he limped home with his head hung low in despair desperately trying to come up with a plausible story to explain why his stringer was empty.

"I got to thinking about all the fish I have caught over the years," he said. "And I came to the conclusion that if I continued bringing home fish at the rate I have been, the rivers would soon run out of fish to catch." The lesser beings with their spinning rods and bottles of salmon eggs looked at him in awe.

Until this point, no one had ever considered the idea that a fish could be hooked, netted, and released, to be caught again another day, and a new religion was born.

"Catch and Release" quickly became the new mantra of serious fishermen, and the mere thought of bringing fish home to the communal frying pan became the eighth deadly sin.

It also became a very convenient way for fisherman who lacked the skills of a perfect presentation of an upstream cast to a rising fish to tell believable stories of all the fish they safely returned to the water. Of course the fish, after being caught so many times, soon learned that once they felt the sting of the hook and the tug of the line, all they had to do was look around for the nearest net, swim into it and return to their favorite big rock in the middle of the river, and wait for a chance to play again.

So began the art of "catch and release" that, along with other environmental issue awareness, preserve and protect our awesome ecosystems and our personal reputations.

OSHA Approved Wilderness

With summer rapidly running towards us, it's time to start thinking about how we are going to survive in the hostile world of Yellowstone country. Believe it or not, there are people out there who honestly believe that taking long moonlight hikes alone in the woods, interacting with large carnivorous meat eaters, and running barefoot through a pine forest are safe things to do. And why shouldn't they?

We have become so accustomed to having mommy and daddy, or the government, standing by to protect us from getting hurt that we assume if there are things out there that are dangerous, someone will be ready with a safety net to make sure we have a good time no matter what stupid things we get ourselves involved in. A box of cue tips comes with a warning about sticking them in our ears; the coffee cup at your friendly neighborhood gas station warns us that the contents may be hot. Once I even saw a sign next to a gas pump warning that gasoline is flammable, and cautioned against striking matches while filling your tank.

There are signs on the highway telling us when we can go fast and when we need to slow down. Signs warning that icy roads may be slick, signs reminding us that pedestrians use cross walks, and even signs telling drivers to avoid head on collisions by yielding to oncoming traffic. My daughter even has a newspaper headline posted on her fridge warning that the government has decided that nuclear war is hazardous to our health.

It could be that we, as a species, are genetically pre-disposed not to be able to take care of ourselves, or recognize that knives are sharp and can cut. If this is a true assumption on my part, I think that maybe a congressional investigation needs to look into ways the wilderness experience can be improved with rules and regulations for wildlife designed to protect us from long claws and sharp teeth.

I am sure that with all the knowledge and experience that already exists within the Occupational Health and Safety Administration, a set of rules and regulations requiring specific safety devices to be installed on all wild animals could be made into law. Maybe puncture proof mittens could be warn by all bears to insure they couldn't grab or scratch unwary tourists. Along with that, a set of stiff fines and penalties could be assessed against any bear that is found to be feeding within one hundred yards of any human activity. Tooth guards for squirrels to prevent biting, venom capture bags for snakes, bells and alarms attached to cougars, and a mandatory vegan diet for wolves, coyotes and other carnivores. The possibilities are endless.

Also, lets not forget that the forest contains trees and trees fall down. Think of the economic growth that would accompany the additional employment opportunities provided by requiring scaffolding be installed to insure that all trees remain upright. For me personally, I would like to see a governmental mandated requirement that all pine needles carry a warning label so I would know that they are sharp and will puncture my feet during my shoeless walks on a summer day.

With health care being an issue that is dominating the evening news lately, I would suggest that the Surgeon General's office work closely with OSHA regulators in requiring that all birds wear diapers. Only then can we have a truly safe wilderness experience.

Bath Time at Our House

It would be nice if the Redhead and I were the only two people in our house that needed a bath now and then. There was a time back in our younger days when that was the way it was but I'm not going to talk about that. Nope! That would be one sure way to get myself into trouble and I'm in trouble enough as it is. I certainly don't need to start fires that don't need to be started.

With that out of the way, the two girls currently living in our house are named Zina and Zoë, and they have eight legs between them. That is four legs each that can dig in the mud, run through the ditch, roll in the dirt, and find other indefinable ways of getting dirty.

I don't mean a little bit dirty; you know, a smudge here and a blot there. I'm talking about the kind of dirty that would make the Charlie Browns' friend Pig Pen shine like the morning sun he was so clean.

Guess who it is that gets the high honor of removing all that muck and guck at least a couple times a week. It's most certainly not the

redhead. After all, she might break a nail or get her hair wet or something equally as horrible, like missing the chance to laugh at me trying to dunk them in the kitchen sink without creating the need to mop up the mud on the floor or take a shower myself.

So there I am, trying to wrangle two wiggly, jumpy, nipping dogs while attempting to brush the sticks, weeds, burrs and some kind of unidentifiable goop I don't want to know what it is, out of their hair; I had just dumped them in the sink, and hosed them down in preparation for the shampoo when the redhead remembers she has a doctors appointment in half an hour and we need to be leaving if we are going to get there on time.

Have you ever smelled a wet dog? There was no way I was going to let them anywhere near the car, let alone in it.

With no other options available besides leaving them unsupervised in house, I tethered them in the back yard next to all the mud, guck, grass and weeds they so love to play in. Only this time, they were already soaking wet. And, I didn't give a single thought to what I would be faced with when I got home. Well, maybe a little thought but not enough to ruin my day.

Sure, I had to start all over again when we got home. The kitchen is in worse shape than it has ever been. But now I am through with the dogs. I have placed them in their crates to dry off and have finished cleaning the kitchen. It is my turn in the tub. That is, unless the Redhead decides she wants in first. Then she will use the rest of the hot water and it will be another cold shower for me. But that is okay! Over the years I have sort of got used to them.

The Learning Curve

The girls, as we call our puppies to avoid the name game, have been going to school every Saturday for the last three weeks. Unfortunately, I don't get the opportunity to pack their lunch, put them on a bus and wave goodbye as they disappear down the street, then slip gently into the house for a quiet cup of warming beverage. No! Not a chance.

What I get to do is load two cages in the back of the redhead's Santa Fe, fill a half dozen half empty water bottles with new water, make sure the blankets in the cages are clean and straight, fill my pockets full of doggy treats, and try to catch them after they escape from my grasp and run down the street to meet up with their new best friend, the cop's dog, and annoy the neighbors with their incessant barking while I try to drag them back to the car.

I will never understand why it is so much harder to get two ShihTzus ready for school than it ever was to get my own daughters dressed and out the door. Okay, maybe that was such an easy task for me because I was mostly gone, or had already left for work before they got out of bed. No, they didn't have to get themselves ready. I'm sure the redhead had that task well in hand. Well, maybe with one of them it was easy; the other shared a specific minor handicap with the dogs. She too was plagued with the attention span of a newly born gnat.

But, that was okay! At least, when our daughters were in school, neither the redhead nor I were required to teach the lessons. We didn't have to read the books, write the reports, add the numbers, or remember to go to the bathroom before the bell rang.

With the ShihTzus, I am responsible to remind them to sit, stay, lay down, wait, and the impossible "stay." I'm the one with the pocket full of treats, which are the dog school equivalent to the grade school gold star. I have to remember to reward them only when they get it right, and not simply because they're cute, and yell the correct name when one of them gets it wrong. That tends to confuse everybody, including me.

School is going well though, especially for me. While they are learning to walk next to me while not pulling on their leash, I get to learn not to yank them back into submission. It really irritates the professional trainer when I do that, and she can bark louder than the dogs. But she is sweet, and always smiles while showing me the approved way to correct my own or my dogs unruly behavior. I'm never really quite sure who is learning, the girls or me.

There is an upside to it all: I have lost about five pounds chasing the pups up and down the street. I get to do deep knee bends getting down to their level to offer them their gold star. And, I am honing my somewhat lacking social skills while apologizing to the neighbors for the little surprise one of them left in the middle of the sidewalk.

Patience! Did I mention patience? It takes a lot of patience to get through the training. At least that is what I think the redhead meant when she said she was losing patience with me when she sees the dogs telling me what they should be doing.

The End is Near

It's sad to say but our time to visit Yellowstone is about to end. I'm sure that everybody has been following the news reports about all the bad things that have been happening inside the park. If you haven't, you need to start paying attention.

It's hard to get around the stories about bison running for their lives to escape an impending cataclysm of sorts that will end vacations of thousands of visitors from around the world. Maybe even bring to an end the lifestyle we have enjoyed all summer. Even the ducks and geese have deserted the park and are taking temporary refuge in the safety of the fields next to my house. Well, maybe not as safe as they would like it to be with all the shotgun blasts that serve as my personal alarm clock in the mornings.

We know that we live on or near one of the largest active volcano's on the planet. But, did you know that there are places where the ground is so hot that way down deep water flashes to steam and explodes hundreds of feet into the air? And, that there are places where mud boils and bubbles like a pot of oatmeal left on the stove too long? Goodness gracious! What is happening?

Okay, maybe the bison running down the road in no particular direction is just their way of attempting to locate a car they can stand in front of for no apparent reason other then to stare at the driver. Or maybe they are running somewhere to find grass that hasn't been eaten by someone else and will give them strength to survive the coming days.

Bison aren't the only ones leaving the park in a big hurry. I didn't make any videos to post of You Tube but I have personally witnessed the exodus of hundreds of Winnebagos, large and small, moving south through the construction area on US20. The markings on their bumpers indicate they may be fleeing to the relative safety of someplace called Utah or California. Some say they are hoping to arrive safely in the mystical land of Havasu, where the Mimosas flow, the cactus grows, and the sun blazes down all day. The profits of doom have announced that over the road traffic into Yellowstone from West Yellowstone will end on November.

As for me, I don't plan to run screaming and flailing my arms into an unsure future. I have no intention of dressing in sackcloth and sandals while parading up and down the street warning the unwary that the end is near. I will stand firm, wrap myself in mukluks and a heavy parka while waiting patiently for the gates to close marking the official end to another good year.

The key to being able to survive any adversity from the Zombie apocalypse to the winter closure of Yellowstone is to be prepared.

My camera batteries are charged, the redhead's car is full of gas, and motel reservations have been made. The only thing that will keep me from being in the park on the third of November, the day it closes for the season, is if it decides to blow up on November second.

In that case, I guess I will wish I were battling tsunamis with my brother Fearless who lives on a beach in Southern California.

Croak

There is a story we all read when we were children about an old Norwegian fisherman who once caught a magical talking fish that promised to grant him any wish he wanted if he would just let him go. As a child, and being somewhat gullible, I wanted to believe the story but had trouble with the concept of a talking fish. Then I met Jim.

About a week ago I was going through my daily cardio exercise routine of flipping the handle of my lounge chair from reclining to upright when the phone rang. I was only slightly irritated by this unwanted intrusion into my focus on better health so I snatched it out of the charger and with my best deep growl I answered it with a gruff, "what do you want?" Almost immediately, a voice spoke a single raspy word.

"Croak!"

On hearing that one sound my heart began pounding in my chest, I broke into a cold sweat and I nearly passed out from fear. It has been over forty years since I last received that message inviting me to load my fishing gear onto my motorcycle and meet my friend Jim for a night of surf fishing. Our favorite finny creature on these late night trips was the Micropogonias undulates, more commonly known as a croaker because of the unique sound it made when you caught one.

I'm not going to go into a long explanation of the secret language Jim and I shared or why going after a fish that made noises when you caught one is important. I will tell you that there is nothing outside the bond of friendship that would drive two grown men to cast a hook into the surf of an in-coming tide at two o'clock in the morning for no other reason than to see who can fill their cooler first.

As it turned out, it wasn't Jim calling from the great beyond as I first thought; it was his son Jeremy calling me from Provo. He didn't want to go fishing for croakers like his dad and I would want to do. He just wanted to know if the Redhead and I would like to come down to Idaho Falls next week and visit with him, his brother and sister, and his mother.

Friendship is the most important gift we can receive, and should never be taken for granted. Jim and I only hung out together for about eighteen months while we were going to school in Florida but in that brief time we built a friendship that continues today, even though he has been gone for several years now.

It's always hard when a friend is lost, especially when you are not there and you can do nothing about it. It's even harder when you don't understand why a part of you has been removed without your permission.

In time I came to understand that as long as there are memories the friendship stays alive. I have many memories of this good and honorable man, and because of that, my friend isn't really gone. I'm sure he is out there somewhere trying to convince some old Norwegian fisherman into believing that fish can talk.

"Croak."

Never Forget

Ten years ago I sat in front of my television set and watched my world change forever. It's not my place to present a history lecture about what happened or speculate on the why. I'll leave that to the historians, political pundits and the talking heads on cable news. I'm just this guy who sat in my living room and witnessed my world come apart, then cried along with millions of others when the towers fell.

During the days following the worst terrorist attack in our country's history, I witnessed a divided nation come together in a common cause. A few exceptions, it didn't seem to matter which political party we belonged to, what the color of our skin happened to be, or what church we worshiped in, we were all Americans. We were wounded deeply, but had a desire to prove to the world that we were not defeated.

Like many others I wanted to show the world who I was, and what my country meant to me, so I started looking for U.S. flags I could display in my yard, office, and from the radio antenna on my truck. None could be found in any of the local stores because they were already attached to windows and bumpers of everything from Cadillac's to pickups driving up and down main streets across the country. Flags were flying everywhere.

When I retired from the Navy I was presented with a flag that under normal circumstance would have remained folded and displayed in a special box on a shelf in my home as a memento of my naval service. The day after the attacks, it was displayed from a homemade flagpole in front of my house, partly to show my neighbors that I was a proud American, and partly as a warning to anyone who dared to do harm to my home or my family.

In time, the initial shock of the attack faded and was replaced with an anger that came from deep down in a dark place that I didn't know existed. I wanted to hurt someone. I wanted to hurt them real bad, and at the time it really didn't matter who it was.

But it's hard to harbor that much anger while witnessing the strength and solidarity of your neighbors and strangers alike as they comforted each other through the love of their country, the meaning of what it is to be an American.

It would be nice if we could go back to the way things were before the attacks but it isn't going to happen. We have learned all too well that we are not as invincible as we thought we were, and will always have to remain on guard against those who would like to destroy us.

Even more important to me is that we must also remember how we came together after the attacks as one people united against a common enemy. If we can remember that during the coming election season, maybe we can find ways to be civil towards each other while taking part in the one thing the terrorists both envy and fear the most about us, our right to voice an opinion, and vote.

May we, under God, protect and preserve our nation, lest we forget.

Printed in the United States
By Bookmasters